A VALENTINE TO REMEMBER

One day they will never forget!

A DATE WITH HER VALENTINE DOC
by Melanie Milburne

Bertie Clark really *shouldn't* be fantasising
about Dr Matt Bishop—he's her boss, and is
100% off-limits! But, working on the hospital's
St Valentine's Day Ball with him, Bertie knows
she can't ignore the sparks flying around
for ever—surely a girl deserves a little fun?

IT HAPPENED IN PARIS…
by Robin Gianna

Biochemical engineer Avery Girard might have
sworn off men, but she can't help but get
swept away by the beauty, magic and romance
of Valentine's Day in Paris…especially when
she's spending it with totally irresistible
Dr Jack Dunbar. One little fling can't hurt, *right*?

**Fall in love this Valentine's Day
with these sparkling romances
available from February 2015!**

Dear Reader

The question I am asked most frequently is: *Where do you get your ideas?* It's not always easy to answer as inspiration for stories can be a deeply subconscious thing and I often don't have a clue where the idea came from. But in the case of Bertie and Matt's story I know exactly what inspired it.

On St Valentine's Day in 2014 I was interviewed on national television about 'How to Write a Best-Selling Romance Novel'. One of the panel hosts, Joe Hildebrand, had recently published *An Average Joe*, a memoir of his quirky childhood, and I just happened to be reading it at the time of the interview—which was kind of spooky! But then, Bertie's mother would say that was the stars or the planets aligning, or something. :)

Last year I was asked to write a short story for *The Australian Review of Fiction* (the first romance author ever to contribute—yay!). I wrote EM AND EM in the first person and couldn't wait to do it again in a full novel, so when my lovely editor Flo Nicoll offered me a chance to write a special St Valentine's Day book I jumped at it—but on the proviso that I could do it in the first person.

I hope you enjoy Bertie and Matt's story as much as I enjoyed writing it. BTW—watch out for Bertie's sister Jem's story, coming soon in Mills & Boon® Medical Romance™!

Best wishes

Melanie Milburne x

A DATE
WITH HER
VALENTINE DOC

BY
MELANIE MILBURNE

Published in Great Britain 2015
by Mills & Boon, an imprint of Harlequin (UK) Limited,
Eton House, 18-24 Paradise Road, Richmond, Surrey, TW9 1SR

© 2015 Melanie Milburne

ISBN: 978-0-263-25934-6

Harlequi
renewab
sustainab
to the leg

Printed a
by CPI A

From as soon as **Melanie Milburne** could pick up a pen she knew she wanted to write. It was when she picked up her first Mills & Boon® at seventeen that she realised she wanted to write romance. After being distracted for a few years by meeting and marrying her own handsome hero, surgeon husband Steve, and having two boys, plus completing a master's of education and becoming a nationally ranked athlete (masters swimming), she decided to write. Five submissions later she sold her first book and is now a multi-published, bestselling, award-winning *USA TODAY* author. In 2008 she won the Australian Readers' Association most popular category/series romance, and in 2011 she won the prestigious Romance Writers of Australia R*BY award.

Melanie loves to hear from her readers via her website, www.melaniemilburne.com.au, or on Facebook: www.facebook.com/melanie.milburne

Recent titles by Melanie Milburne:

FLIRTING WITH THE SOCIALITE DOC
DR CHANDLER'S SLEEPING BEAUTY
SYDNEY HARBOUR HOSPITAL: LEXI'S SECRET
THE SURGEON SHE NEVER FORGOT
THE MAN WITH THE LOCKED AWAY HEART

These books are also available in eBook format from www.millsandboon.co.uk

Each year I am part of the silent auction
for the Heart Foundation in Tasmania. I offer a
book dedication and this year's winner was Maria Chung,
who wanted this book to be dedicated to her husband:

Dr Stephen Chung, a wonderful husband, father and doctor.

Thank you to both of you for your continued support
of the Heart Foundation in Tasmania.

MM

**Praise for
Melanie Milburne:**

'Fast-paced, passionate and simply irresistible,
SYDNEY HARBOUR HOSPITAL: LEXI'S SECRET is a
powerful tale of redemption, hope and second chances that
sparkles with richly drawn characters, warm-hearted pathos,
tender emotion, sizzling sensuality and uplifting romance.'
—*CataRomance*

'A tale of new beginnings, redemption and hope that
will make readers chuckle as well as wipe away a tear.
A compelling medical drama about letting go of the past
and seizing the day, it is fast-paced and sparkles with
mesmerising emotion and intense passion.'
—*GoodReads* on
THEIR MOST FORBIDDEN FLING

CHAPTER ONE

THE FIRST THING I saw when I walked into the ICU office on my first day back to work after my honeymoon was my postcard pinned to the noticeboard. Well, it was *supposed* to be my honeymoon. I'd booked the leave for months ahead. It's hard to get three weeks off in a row at St Ignatius, especially before Christmas. There are a lot of working mums at St Iggy's and I always feel guilty if I'm stuffing up someone's plan to be at their little kid's Christmas concert. Which was why I hadn't come back to work until the 'honeymoon' was over, so to speak.

My postcard was right in the centre of the noticeboard. In pride of place. Flashing like a beacon. The last time I'd seen it had been in my chalet room at the ski resort in Italy, along with two others I'd written to my elderly neighbours. I swear I hadn't actually intended to post them. It had been a therapeutic exercise my mother had suggested to rid myself of negative energy, but the super-efficient housekeeping staff must have seen them lying on the desk and helpfully posted them for me. That's service for you.

If I turned that wretched postcard around I would

see the lies I'd scrawled there after consuming a lonely cocktail or two…actually, I think it was three. *All went amazingly well! Having an awesome time!*

Now that I look back with twenty-twenty hindsight I can see all the signs. The red flags and the faintly ringing alarm bells I ignored at the time. I hate to sound like a cliché but I really was the last person to know. My mother said she knew the first time she met Andy. It was his aura that gave him away. My dad said three of Andy's chakras were blocked. My sister Jem said it was because he was a twat.

I guess they were all right in the end.

The chance to get rid of the postcard escaped me when Jill, the ward clerk, came in behind me with a couple of residents and chorused, 'Here's the blushing bride!' I was blushing all right. Big time. Looking at that sea of smiling faces, I didn't have the heart or the courage to tell them the wedding hadn't gone ahead. I smiled inanely and made some excuse about seeing an elderly patient and scooted out of there. I had only been at St Iggy's a little less than a year so I didn't know anyone well enough to consider them close friends, although some of the girls were really nice, Gracie McCurcher— one of the intensive care nurses—in particular.

And as to anyone finding out on social media, I'd closed my profile page a couple of years ago after someone had hacked into my account and used my image in a porn ad. Try explaining *that* to your workmates, especially the male ones.

My home village in Yorkshire is a long way from London—in more ways than one, but more on that later—so I figured it didn't matter if I didn't tell everyone I'd got dumped the night before the wedding. Cowardly, I know, but, to tell you the truth, I was still trying to get used to being single. Andy and I were together—not actually living together, because I'm idiotically old-fashioned, which is ironic when you consider my unconventional upbringing—for five and a half years.

I know what you're thinking. How could I *not* have known he wasn't in love with me after all that time? I'm not sure how to answer. I loved him so I expected him to love me back. Naïve of me perhaps but that's just the way I'm made. But maybe on some level I'd always known he was marking time until someone better came along.

I stood by the bedside of Mr Simmons, a long-term elderly patient, on that cold and dismal January morning and watched as he quietly slipped away. There is something incredibly sacred about watching someone die. Mind you, it's not always peaceful. Some struggle as if they aren't quite ready to leave their loved ones. Others slip away on a soundless sigh the moment their absent loved one arrives. It's as if they've waited until that moment of contact to finally let go. I've lost count of how many deaths I've seen. But I guess that's one of the downsides of working in ICU. Not everyone walks out with a smile on his or her face. Not everyone walks out, period.

I can cope with the death of an elderly person like Mr Simmons. I can even manage with a middle-aged person's death if they've lived a full and happy life and are surrounded by the people they love. It's the kids that get me. Babies in particular. It seems so unfair they don't get a chance to have a go at screwing up their life like I've screwed up mine.

Mr Simmons's grandchildren and great-grandchildren had been in the night before and said their final good-byes. His wife died a couple of years ago so there was only his son and daughter by his bed. I watched as they each kissed his forehead, and then stroked his papery hand, and each shed a tear or two for the long and happy life that was coming to a close.

ICU is a pretty public place to die, which was why I had wrangled for months with the CEO to give me a quiet corner—if there is such a thing in an ICU department—so relatives could spend an hour or two without nurses or orderlies or whatever interrupting their last moments with their loved one. I had even had special permission granted to light candles of reflection and operate an aromatherapy infusion machine so the patients and their relatives and friends could breathe in their favourite scents instead of the smell of hospital-grade antiseptic.

Because it was my baby, while I'd been away things had fallen a little by the wayside, but I was back now and intent on finalising the introduction of my stress cost abatement model. I proposed to show how improving the environment in which relatives experienced illness or death in ICU ultimately reduced costs to the hospital—less demand for later counselling, reduced incidence and costs of litigation, and even reduced stress leave for ICU staff. I planned to present it at an upcoming hospital management meeting because I knew I could prove there would be benefits to the whole department with reduced stress in the ICU environment, not just for patients but for staff as well.

I softly closed the door—yes, not a curtain but an actual door!—on the grieving relatives and headed back to the glassed-in office where the registrars, interns and residents were being briefed by one of the consultants. I hadn't yet met the new director. He'd started the day after I'd left for my…erm…break.

I was looking at the back view of the consultant. At first I thought it was Professor Cleary—we call him Professor Dreary behind his back because he's such a pessimist—but when I got closer I realised it was some-one much younger. He had very broad shoulders and he was tall. I mean *really* tall. He was at least a couple of inches taller than the registrar, Mark Jones, who we affectionately call Lurch.

I'm not sure if someone said I was coming over or whether the new director heard me approach. But he suddenly turned and his eyes met mine. Something fizzed in the air like a stray current of electricity. I actually felt the hairs on the back of my neck lift up. I had never seen such startling grey-blue eyes. Pierc-ing and intense, intelligent and incisive, they looked at me in a frank and assessing manner I found distinctly unnerving.

'Dr Clark?'

'Bertie,' I said with a smile that felt a little forced. 'It's short for Beatrix with an X.'

He stood there looking down at me as if I were a strange oddity he'd never encountered in ICU before. I wondered if it was my hairstyle. I have longish wavy honey-brown hair, which I like to keep under some semblance of control when I'm working. That morning I'd tied it in two round knots either side of my head like teddy-bear ears.

Or maybe it was my outfit that had caused that quizzical frown to appear between his eyes. I'm the first to admit I'm a little out there in my choice of clothing. No white coat—not that we doctors wear them any more—or scrubs for me unless I've come from Theatre. I like colour and lots of it. It can have a powerful effect on patients' moods, particularly children. Besides, all you ever see in winter is black and brown and grey. That morning I had on skinny-leg pink jeans and a pea-green jumper with blue frogs on it. The new director glanced at the frogs on my breasts before returning his gaze to mine. Something closed off at the back of his eyes, as if he were pulling up a screen.

I didn't offer him my hand but, then, he didn't offer his. I'm normally a polite person but I wasn't sure I wanted to touch him until I had better control of myself. If his gaze could make me feel like I'd walked in wearing a string bikini then what would his touch do?

'Matt Bishop,' he said in a deep, mellifluous baritone that had an odd effect on the base of my spine. It felt loose…unhinged. 'I'd like to see you in my office.' He glanced at his watch before zapping me again with his gaze. 'Five minutes.'

I watched as he strode away, effectively dismissing me as if I was nothing but a lowly serf. Who the hell did he think he was, ordering me about like a medical student? I was as qualified as him. Well, almost.

I was aware of the staff's collective gaze as the air rippled with tension in his wake.

'You'd better not be late, Bertie,' Jill, the ward clerk, said. 'He's a stickler for punctuality. Alex Kingston got hauled over the coals for showing up two minutes late for a ward round.'

Gracie McCurcher gave a grimace and huddled further into the office chair she was swivelling on. 'He's nothing like Jeffrey, is he?'

Jeffrey Hooper was our previous director. He retired the week before I left for my...holiday. Think benevolent uncle or godparent. Jeffrey was the kindest, most supportive ICU specialist I've ever come across. He could be gruff at times but everyone knew his bark was just a front.

'That's part of the problem,' Jill said. 'Jeffrey was too lax in running this department. The costs have blown out and now Dr Bishop has to rein everything in. I don't envy him. He's not going to make any friends doing it, that I can tell you.'

I moved my lips back and forth and up and down. My sister Jem calls it my bunny-rabbit twitch. I do it when I'm stressed. Which is kind of embarrassing when my whole research project is on reducing stress. I'm supposed to be the poster girl for serenity. But the truth is I'm like the ducks on the Serpentine in Hyde Park. They look like they're floating effortlessly on the surface but underneath the water their little webbed feet are paddling like crazy.

'You'd better keep the photos until after work,' Gracie said.

Photos? I thought. Oh, *those* photos. I pasted on a smile that made my face ache. Everyone was looking at me. Here was my chance to come clean. To tell them there hadn't been a wedding. I could see my postcard out of the corner of my eye. It was still in pride of place on the noticeboard. Hadn't anyone else been on holiday, for God's sake? I'm not sure how long I stood there with my mouth stretched in that rictus smile but it felt longer than my 'honeymoon'. I wondered if I could edit some wedding-ish snaps on my phone. Set up a temporary social network account or something. It would give me some breathing space until I plucked up the courage to tell the truth.

'Good suggestion,' I said, and, taking a deep breath, headed to the lion's den.

I gave the closed door a quick rap and winced as my knuckles protested. It was a timely reminder I would need to develop a thicker skin if I were to survive the next few rounds with Dr Matt Bishop.

'Come in.'

I walked into his office but it was nothing like his predecessor had left it. Gone were the lopsided towers of files and patient notes and budgetary reports. There were no family photos on the cluttered desk. No empty or half-drunk cups of coffee. No cookie crumbs. No glass jar full of colourful dental-filling-pulling sweets. The office had been stripped bare of its character. It was as sterile and as cool as the man who sat behind the acre of desk.

'Close the door.'

I paused, giving him an arch look. I might have had an alternative upbringing but at least my parents taught me the magic word.

'Please,' he added, with a smidgeon of a lip curl.

Round one to me, I thought.

The door clicked shut and I moved a little closer to the desk. The closer I got the more my skin prickled. It was like entering a no-go zone monitored by invisible radar.

I wondered what my mum would make of his aura. Matt Bishop had a firm mouth that looked like it wasn't used to smiling. His jaw had a determined set to it as if he was unfamiliar with the notion of compromise. His skin was olive toned but it looked as if he hadn't been anywhere with strong sunshine for several months…but, then, that's our English summer for you. His hair was a rich, dark brown, thick and plentiful but cut short in a no-nonsense style. He was closely shaven and in the air I could pick up a faint trace of lime and lemongrass, a light, fresh scent that made my nostrils widen in appreciation. I'm a sucker for subtle aftershave.

I hate stepping into the lift with a bunch of young male medical students who've gone crazy with those cheap aerosol body sprays. I once had to hold my breath for six floors and the lift stopped on every one. I was wheezing like I had emphysema by the time I got out.

My mum reckons she can read auras. I'm more of a wardrobe reader. Matt Bishop was wearing a crisply ironed white shirt with a black and silver striped tie with a Windsor knot and black trousers with knife-edge pleats that spoke of a man who preferred formality to casual friendliness. But to counter that the sleeves of his shirt were folded back past his wrists, revealing strong forearms with a generous sprinkling of dark hair that went all the way down to his hands and along each of his long fingers. His nails were neat and square, unlike mine, which had suffered the fallout of the last two weeks after months of coaxing them to grow, and were now back to their nibbled-to-the-quick state.

I curled my fingers into my palms in case he noticed and sat down in the chair opposite his desk. I sat not because he told me to. He didn't. I sat because I didn't care for the schoolgirl-called-into-the-headmaster's-office dynamic he had going on. It was much better to be seated so I could look at him on the level. Mind you, with his considerable height advantage I would have had to be sitting on a stack of medical textbooks to be eye to eye with him.

His unreadable gaze meshed with mine. 'I believe congratulations are in order.'

'Erm…yes,' I said. What else could I say? No, I found my fiancé in bed with one of the bridesmaids' sister the night before the wedding? And that *he* dumped me before I could get in first? And how I tipsily wrote postcards that were subsequently sent about what a fabulous time I was having on my honeymoon? Not going to happen. Not to Matt Bishop anyway. I would tell people on a need-to-know basis and right now no one needed to know.

I *needed* no one to know.

There was a pregnant silence.

I got the feeling he was waiting for me to fill it, though with what I'm not sure. Did he want me to tell him where I went on my honeymoon? What I wore? Who caught the bouquet? I thought men weren't all that interested in weddings, even when it was their own.

I stared back at him with my heart beating like a hummingbird had got trapped in one of my valves. *You could tell him.* The thought slipped under the locked door of my resolve. *No way!* the other side of my brain threw back. It was like a tennis match was going on inside my head. I was so flustered by it I shifted in my seat as if there were thumbtacks poking into my jeans.

His eyes drilled into mine. 'Is everything all right?'

'Yes.' I smiled stiffly. 'Sure. Fine. Absolutely.'

Another silence passed.

Here's the thing. I'm not good with silences. They freak me out. It's because my parents went through a no-speaking phase when Jem and I were kids. They wanted us to pretend we were living in an abbey like at Mont Saint Michel in Normandy in France, where talking is banned in order to concentrate on prayer. It would have helped if they'd taught us sign language first. Thankfully it didn't last long but it's left its mark. I have this tendency to talk inanely if there's even a hint of a break in the conversation.

'So, how are you liking St Iggy's so far?' I said. 'Isn't it a nice place? Everyone's so friendly and—'

'Harrison Redding, the CEO, tells me you're doing a research project on stress reduction,' Matt Bishop said.

'Yes,' I said. As much as I didn't care for his clipped tone, at least I was back on safer ground. I mentally wiped my brow. Phew! I could talk all day about my project. 'I'm looking at ways of mitigating the stress on patients, relatives and staff when a patient is in ICU, in particular when a patient is facing death. Stress is a costly burden to the unit. Staff take weeks—sometimes months—of stress leave when cases are difficult to handle. Patients lodge unnecessary and career-damaging lawsuits when they feel sidelined or their expectations aren't met. My aim is to show how using various stress intervention programmes and some physical ways of reducing stress, such as aromas and music tones and other environmental changes, can significantly reduce that cost to the hospital. My stress cost abatement model will help both staff and patients and their loved ones deal better with their situation.'

I waited for his response...and waited.

After what seemed like a week he leaned forward and put his forearms on the desk and loosely interlaced his fingers. 'You've had ethics approval?'

'Of course.'

I watched as he slowly flicked one of his thumbs against the other. Flick. Flick. Flick. I tried to read his expression but he could have been sitting at a poker tournament. Nothing moved on his face, not even a muscle. I was having trouble keeping my nervous bunny twitch under control. I could feel it building inside me like the urge to sneeze.

His eyes bored into mine. 'I have some issues with your project.'

I blinked. 'Pardon?'

'I'm not convinced this unit can afford the space you've been allocated,' he said. 'I understand Dr Hooper was the one to approve the end room for your use?'

'Yes, but the CEO was also—'

'And the room next to the relatives' room?'

'Yes, because I felt it was important to give people a choice in—'

'What sort of data have you produced so far?'

I wished I hadn't gone on leave for more reasons than the obvious one. It felt like ages since I'd looked at my data. Most of it was descriptive, which was something the survey questionnaire over the next few critical weeks would address. I understood the scientific method. Data had to be controlled, repeatable and sufficient; otherwise, it was useless. But I also wanted a chance to change the thinking around death and dying. Everyone was so frightened of it, which produced enormous amounts of stress. 'I'm still collecting data from patient and staff surveys,' I said. 'I have a series of interviews to do, which will also be recorded and collated.'

I wasn't too keen on the sceptical glint in his eyes. 'Multiplication of anecdotes is not data, Dr Clark.'

I silently ground my teeth…or at least I tried to be silent. Jem says she can always hear me because she listened to it for years when we shared a bedroom when we were kids. Apparently I do it in my sleep.

I *so* did not need this right now. I had enough on my plate in my private life, without my professional life going down the toilet as well. I understood how Matt Bishop was in brisk and efficient new broom mode. I understood the pressure of coming in on budget, especially when you'd inherited a mess not of your own making. But I wasn't going to be intimidated by a man who had taken an instant dislike to me for how I dressed or wore my hair.

He would have to get over himself. *I* wasn't changing.

'Will that be all, Dr Bishop?' I asked in mock meekness as I rose from the chair. 'I have some pre-assessments to see to on the ward.'

This time a muscle did move in his jaw. In and out like a miniature hammer. A hard sheen came over his gaze as it held mine—an impenetrable layer of antagonism that dared me to lock horns with him. I'm not normally one to pick fights but I resented the way he'd spoken to me as if I were a lazy high-school student who hadn't done their homework. If he wanted a fight then I would give him one.

I felt a frisson pass through my body, an electric current that made my nerves flutter and dance. I can't remember a time when I felt more switched on. It was like someone had plugged me into a live socket. My entire body was vibrating with energy, a restless and vibrant energy it had never felt before.

Without relaxing his hold on my gaze, he reached for a sheet of paper on the desk in front of him, which I presumed was an outline of my research. His top lip lifted in a sardonic arc. 'Your project name has a rather unfortunate acronym, don't you think?'

I looked at him blankly for a moment. And then I got it. I was annoyed I hadn't realised it before. Stress Cost Abatement Model. S.C.A.M. Why on earth hadn't someone pointed it out earlier? I felt like an idiot. Would everyone be snickering at me once Matt Bishop shared his observation around the water cooler? My stomach knotted. Maybe they already were... Was that why everyone had looked at me when I came to the office just now? Had they been talking about me...*laughing* at me?

I was incensed. Livid to the point of exploding with anger so intense it felt like it was bursting out of each and every corpuscle of my blood. I could feel the heat in my cheeks burning like the bars of a two-thousand-watt radiator. I had spent most of my childhood being sniggered at for my unconventional background. How would I ever be taken seriously professionally once this did the rounds?

I don't often lose my temper, but when I do it's like all those years of keeping my thoughts and opinions to myself come spilling out in a shrieking tirade that I can't stop once I get started. It's like trying to put a champagne cork back in the bottle.

I hissed in a breath and released it in a rush. 'I *detest* men like you. You think just because you've been appointed director you can brandish your power about like a smart-ass kid with a new toy. You think your colleagues are dumb old chess pieces you can push around as you please. Well, I have news for you, Dr Bishop. This is one chess piece you can't screw around with.'

I probably shouldn't have used *that* particular word. The connotation of it changed the atmosphere from electric to erotic. I could feel it thrumming in the air. I could see the glint of it in his grey-blue gaze as it tussled with mine. I'm not sure where his mind was going, but I knew what images mine was conjuring up—X-rated ones. Naked bodies. His and mine. Writhing around on a bed in the throes of animal passion.

Thing is…it's been ages since I've had sex. I'm pretty sure that's why my mind was running off the way it was. I'd put Andy's lack of interest over the last couple of months down to busyness with work as a stock analyst. I put down my own to lack of interest, period. I blamed it on the contraceptive pill I'd been taking. But then I changed pills and I was exactly the same. Go figure.

I saw Matt Bishop's eyes take in my scorching cheeks and then he lowered his gaze to my mouth. It was only for a moment but I felt as if he had touched me with a searing brand. I bit my tongue to keep it from moistening my lips but that meant I couldn't say anything to break the throbbing silence. Not that I was going to apologise or anything. As far as I was concerned, he'd asked for a verbal spray and, given another chance, I would give him one again.

He sat back in his chair, his eyes holding mine in a lock that made the backs of my knees feel fizzy. It took an enormous effort on my part not to look away. I had an unnerving feeling he could see through my brief flash of anger—the overly defensive front that disguised my feelings of inadequacy. I'd spent most of my life hiding my insecurities but I got the sense he could read every micro-expression on my face, even the ones I thought I wasn't expressing. His gaze was so steady, so watchful and so intuitive I was sure he was reading every thought that was running through my mind, including—even more unsettling—the X-rated ones.

'I'll keep that in mind,' he said. 'Close the door on your way out.' He waited a beat before he added with an enigmatic half-smile, '*Please*.'

CHAPTER TWO

I FINISHED MY pre-assessment clinic and walked back to ICU. Stalked would be more accurate. I was still brooding over Matt Bishop's treatment of me. Why had he taken such a set against me? I wasn't used to making instant enemies. I considered myself an easygoing person who got on with everyone. Mostly.

Come to think of it, there have been a couple of times when I've run up against someone who didn't share my take on things. Like my neighbour, who kept spraying the other neighbour's cat with a hose every time it came into his garden. That's just plain cruel and I didn't refrain from telling him so. I got myself hosed for my trouble, but at least I felt good about standing up for Ginger.

And then there was the guy who'd been ripping off another elderly neighbour a few doors down. Elsie Montgomery employed him to do some gardening and odd jobs but it wasn't long before he was doing her shopping and taking her to the doctor or on other outings. At first I thought he was doing it out of the goodness of his heart, but then I found out from Elsie—reluctantly, because she was embarrassed—he had been taking money out of her bank account after he'd got her to tell him her PIN.

I wanted Elsie to press charges against him for elder abuse but she thought he'd been punished enough by me shouting at him in the street in front of all the neighbours. That and the naming-and-shaming leaflet drop. That was a stroke of genius on my part. I got a team of local kids to help me distribute them. It will be a long time before he gets to cut any lawns in our suburb, possibly the whole country.

I was walking past the staff change rooms when Gracie appeared. 'How did it go? What did he say to you?'

I rolled my eyes. 'He has issues with my project.'

'What sort of issues?'

I gave her a disgruntled look. I wasn't going to spell it out for her. Word would spread fast enough. 'The rooms I've been allocated, for one thing. He thinks we can't afford the space.'

Gracie frowned. 'But you're doing amazing things with the patients and families. Everyone says so. Look at what you did for the Matheson family. You brought such comfort to them when they lost their son before Christmas.'

I pictured the Matheson family collected around Daniel's twenty-one-year-old body as he breathed his last breaths after a long and difficult battle against sarcoma. I spent hours with them, preparing them and Daniel for the end. I encouraged them to be open with Daniel about their feelings, not to be ashamed of the anger they were feeling about his life being cut short, but to accept that as a part of the journey through grief. I taught Daniel's father, who was uncomfortable showing emotion or affection, to gently massage his son to help him relax. When Daniel finally passed it was so peaceful in the room you could hear the birds twittering outside.

I let out a breath as we walked along the corridor back to the unit. 'I can't stop now. I'm only just beginning to see results. I've had three nurses tell me how much they got out of the meditation exercise I gave before I went on leave. When nurses get stressed, patients get stressed. It's not rocket science. It's common sense.'

'But surely Dr Bishop can't block your project now,' Gracie said.

I held my hands out for the antiseptic gel from the dispenser on the wall, my mouth set in an indomitable line. 'I'd like to see him try.'

I got busy doing a PICC line for a chemotherapy patient and then I had to help one of the registrars with setting up a patient's ventilator. I was due for Theatre for an afternoon list with one of the neurosurgeons, Stuart McTaggart. Not my favourite person at St Iggy's, but while he had an abrasive personality there was certainly nothing wrong with his surgical skills. Patients came from all over the country to see him. He had a world-class reputation for neurosurgery and was considered to be one of the best neurosurgeons of his generation.

I went to the doctors' room to grab a quick bite of lunch. It was a medium-sized room big enough for a six-person dining table and chairs, a couple of mismatched armchairs, a coffee table, a sink and a small fridge. The daily newspapers were spread out on the table, where a bowl of fruit acted as a paperweight.

Personally, I thought the place could do with a face-lift, maybe a bit of feng shui wouldn't go astray, but I was fairly new on staff, considering some people had been here for their entire careers, so I picked my battles.

I reached for an apple out of the bowl as the door opened. I looked up to see Matt Bishop enter the staff-room. His expression showed no surprise or discomfit at seeing me there. In fact, I thought I caught a glimmer of a smile lurking in his eyes. No doubt he was still enjoying the joke he'd made of my project. I hadn't heard anyone say anything about it so far but I knew it wouldn't be long before they did. He wouldn't be able to keep such a gem of hilarity to himself.

I felt my anger go up another notch. Why did I attract this sort of stuff? Why couldn't I go about my life without people making fun of me? Now, you might ask why would a girl wear bright, fun clothes and twist her hair into wacky hairstyles if she was afraid of people laughing at her? Duh! If they're laughing at my clothes and my hair I don't have to feel they're laughing at *me*. There's a difference and to me it's a big one.

I bit into the apple with a loud crunch. I was down a round and I had some serious catching up to do. I chewed the mouthful and then took another. And another. It wasn't the nicest apple, to tell you the truth. But I was committed now so I had to finish it. I can be stubborn at times—most of the time, to be honest. I *hate* giving in. I hate being defeated by something or someone. I'd spent a lot of my childhood being bullied so I guess that's why. It's not just about losing face. I hate failure. It goes against my nature. I'm positive in my outlook. I go into things expecting to achieve my mission. I don't let the naysayers get to me...or I try not to.

'So where did you go on honeymoon?' Matt Bishop asked, just as I'd taken another mouthful.

I swear to God I almost choked on that piece of apple. I thought he'd have to give me the Heimlich manoeuvre—not that we do that any more, but still. I coughed and spluttered, my eyes streaming, my cheeks as red as the skin of the piece of apple I was trying to shift from my airway.

He stepped towards me. 'Are you okay?'

I signalled with one of my hands that I was fine. He waited patiently with his steady gaze trained on mine. Of course I couldn't pretend I was choking forever, and since—technically speaking—I had been on honeymoon/ holiday I decided to stay as close to the truth as possible once I got my airway clear. 'Skiing...Italy.'

'Where in Italy?'

'Livigno.'

He acknowledged that with a slight nod as he reached for a coffee cup. 'Good choice.'

I put the rest of my apple in the bin. It wasn't my choice. I'm a hopeless skier. I'd only agreed to it because it was what Andy wanted. And rather than waste the money—because he hadn't paid the travel insurance as I'd asked him to—I'd doggedly stuck with the plan. I must admit I was proud of myself in that I progressed off the nursery slopes, but not very far. 'You ski?' I asked.

'Occasionally.'

There was a silence broken only by the sound of coffee being poured into his cup. I waited to see if he put milk or sugar or sweetener in it. You've guessed it. There's a lot you can tell about someone from how they take their coffee. He was a straight-up man. No added extras. And he drank it smoking hot. I watched as he took his first mouthful without even wincing at the steamy heat.

'What does your husband do?'

The question caught me off guard. I was too busy watching the way his mouth had shaped around the rim of his cup. Why had I thought his mouth hard and uncompromising? He had the sort of mouth that would make Michelangelo dash off for a chisel. The lower lip was sensually full and the top one neatly defined. I don't think I'd ever seen such a beautifully sculpted mouth. I began to wonder what it would feel like pressed to my own...

'Pardon?'

'Is your husband a doctor too?'

Something about the way he said the word 'husband' made me think he was putting it in inverted commas or even in italics. It was the way he stressed the word. That, and the way his mouth got a slight curl to it as if he thought the notion of someone wanting to marry me was hilariously unbelievable.

'No, erm, he's a stock analyst.'

'In London?'

'Yes.'

There's an art to lying and I like to think I'm pretty good at it. After all, I've been doing it all my life. I learned early on not to tell people the truth. Living in a commune with your parents from the age of six sort of does that to you. I wouldn't have lasted long at school if I had Shown and Told some of the things I'd seen and heard.

No, it's not the lying that's the problem. That's the easy part. It's keeping track of them that gets tricky. So far I hadn't strayed too far off the path. Andy was a stock analyst and he worked in London. He was currently seeking a transfer to the New York branch of his firm, which, to be frank, I welcomed wholeheartedly. London is a big city but I didn't fancy running into him and his new girlfriend any time soon. It was bad enough having him come to my house to collect all his things. I made it easy for him by leaving them in the front garden. Yes, I know, it was petty, but I got an enormous sense of satisfaction from throwing them from the second-floor window. It wasn't my fault it had snowed half a metre overnight. I'm not in control of the weather.

I decided in order to keep my lying tally down I had to ask some questions of my own. 'Are you married?'

'No.'

'In a relationship?'

He paused for a nanosecond. 'No.'

I wondered if he had broken up recently, or if the break-up—if there had been one—still hurt. 'Kids?'

He frowned. 'No, of course not.'

'Why of course not?'

'Call me old-fashioned but I like to do things in the right order,' he said.

I tilted my head at him. 'So let me guess…you haven't lived with anyone?'

'No.'

I pondered over that for a moment while he took

a packet of sandwiches from the small fridge and sat down at the table. He opened one of the newspapers on the table and began to eat his sandwiches in what I could only describe as a mechanical way. I'm the first to admit hospital food isn't much to get all excited about, but the sandwiches for the doctors' room were always freshly made and contained healthy ingredients, or at least they had since I'd spoken to the head of catering a few weeks back.

'That's bad for you, you know,' I said. I know it was none of my business what or how he ate but the silence was there and I wanted to fill it. Needed to fill it, more like.

Matt Bishop didn't bother to glance my way. He turned the newspaper page over and reached for another sandwich. 'What is?'

'Eating and reading. At the same time, I mean.'

He sat back in his chair and looked at me with an inscrutable expression. 'You have something against multitasking?'

I didn't let his satirical tone faze me. 'Eating while performing other tasks is a bad habit. It can lead to overeating. You might be full by page three but you keep on eating until you get to the sports page out of habit.'

He closed the newspaper and pushed it to the other side of the table. 'How long were you going out with your *husband* before he asked you to marry him?'

There, he'd done it again. I wasn't imagining it. He'd stressed the word 'husband'. What was with the sudden interest in my private life? Or did he think it impossible anyone could be remotely interested in me? With the end of my engagement so recent I was feeling a bit

fragile in terms of self-esteem. Come to think of it, my
self-esteem has always been a little on the eggshell side.
'Erm, actually, he didn't ask me,' I said. 'I asked him.'

He lifted one of his dark eyebrows. 'Oh?'

'You don't approve.'

'It's none of my business.'

I folded my arms and gave him a look. 'I fail to see
why the man has to have all the power in a relationship.
Why should a girl have to wait months and months, possibly years for a proposal? Living every moment in a
state of will-he-or-won't-he panic?'

'Don't blame me,' he said mildly. 'I didn't write the
rule book.'

I pursed my lips, not my most attractive pose, but
still. Jem calls it my cat's-bottom pout. I had the strang-
est feeling Matt Bishop was smiling behind that unreadable look he was giving me. There was a tiny light in
his eyes that twinkled now and again.

'So how did he take it when you popped the question?' he asked.

'He said yes, obviously.' Not straight away, but I
wasn't going to tell Matt Bishop *that* little detail. Andy
and I had discussed marriage over the years. He just
hadn't got around to formally asking me. I got tired of
waiting. I know it's weird, considering my non-traditional
background, but I really longed to be a proper bride: the
white dress and veil and the church and the flowers and
confetti and the adorable little flower girl and the cute
little pageboy.

My parents had never formally married because they
didn't believe in the institution of marriage—any institution, really. They have an open relationship, which

seems to work for them. Don't ask me how. I've never said anything to them, but every time I looked at the photos of their thirty years of life together I've always felt like something was missing.

Matt picked up his coffee cup and surveyed me as he took another sip. 'How long have you been at St Ignatius?'

'Ten and a half months.'

'Where were you before here?'

'St Thomas',' I said, and tossed the question back, even though I already knew the answer because I'd overheard two of the nurses talking about him in the change room. 'You?'

'I trained in London and spent most of my time at Chelsea and Westminster, apart from the last twelve months in the US.'

I wondered why he had gone abroad and if it had anything to do with a woman, here or over there. I hadn't heard anything about his private life. Word has it he kept it exactly that—private.

My phone beeped with an incoming message and I glanced down to see it was a text from Jem.

How r u doing? it said.

I quickly typed back. Fine.

Within seconds she typed back. What did everyone say?

I typed back. I haven't told them.

She came back with, Y not?

I typed back the emoticon smiley face with red cheeks. She sent me a smiley face with love hearts for eyes. It was times like this I was truly glad I had a sister. She knew me better than anyone. She knew I needed time to sort my feelings out, to get my head around the idea of being single again.

I had a feeling she also knew it was not so much my heart that was broken but my pride. It's not that I didn't love Andy. I loved him from the moment I met him. He was charming and funny and made me feel as if I was the most important person in his life...for about a month. I know all relationships take work and I put in. I really did. It's just he hadn't factored in my career. His always came first. It caused many an argument. I mean, it's not as if someone's going to die if he doesn't show up for work. He never seemed to understand I couldn't take off a day whenever I felt like it because he was bored and wanted company.

I put my phone back in my jeans pocket and met Matt Bishop's inscrutable gaze. I wondered if he could see any of the thought processes of my brain flitting over my face. I like to think I can keep my cards pretty close, but something about his intense grey-blue eyes made me feel exposed, as if all my insecurities and doubts were lined up on show for his perusal.

'Any further questions?' I asked, with a pert look.

He held my look for an extra beat. 'Not at the moment.'

I turned on my heel and scooted out of there. Colour me suspicious, but I had a feeling there was not much that would get past Dr Matt Bishop's sharply intelligent grey-blues.

Theatre was tense but, then, Stuart McTaggart always operated that way. He wasn't one of those surgeons who chatted about what he did on the weekend or how well his kids were doing at Cambridge or Oxford—yadda-yadda-yadda. He didn't have classical music playing, like a couple of the other surgeons on staff did. He insisted on absolute silence, apart from when he had something to say. I'd had to learn early on to button my lips while in Theatre with him. He was gruff to the point of surly and he barked out orders like a drill sergeant. Some of the junior theatre staff found him terrifying. Some of the more senior staff hated working with him.

Funnily enough, I didn't find him too hard to handle. I understood the pressure he was under. Patients were more demanding of good outcomes than in the past, or at least they had better access to legal representation and were more aware of their rights. The litigious climate meant a lot of clinicians at the pointy end of medicine were under far greater pressure and scrutiny than ever before. That could be a good and a bad thing depending on the circumstances. It was part of why I wanted to pursue my research. Reducing the stress of the hospital experience was a win-win for everyone. Apart perhaps from the greedy lawyers, of course, but don't get me started.

Stuart McTaggart was operating on a twenty-seven-year-old man with a very vascular and awkwardly placed benign brain tumour. Jason Ryder was a recently married man with a baby on the way. He was a keen sportsman, playing semi-professional golf. He had collapsed whilst playing in a tournament and been admitted to St Iggy's via A and E. All was going well until he developed a bleed. Alex Kingston, the surgical registrar, was the first to cop the flak from Stuart.

'Suck the blood out of the way, Kingston!' he said. 'I can't diathermy bleeders if they're underwater!'

Next in line was Leanne Griffiths, the scrub nurse.

'Be aware of what's happening in the operation, Sister Griffiths. I can't wait around while you call for more swabs. They should be open, on the table, ready when I need them. Which is now!'

Then it was my turn. Woot. Woot.

'What blood pressure have you got this patient running at, Dr Clark? He looks hypertensive to me and that's not assisting with this blood loss!'

And on it went. Everyone was to blame except Stuart. But, then, really, no one was to blame—it was just the nature of the tumour and the stress of trying to remove it with minimal damage to the normal brain. The human body was not always predictable. Things didn't always work out. They weren't working out now. The only way to eventually stop the haemorrhage was to ligate a couple of largish vessels, causing irreparable damage to a large part of what had been a normal brain.

The person I'd anaesthetised wasn't going to be the person who woke up…if he woke up. I hated even *thinking* those words. I always focussed on the positive. It gave great comfort to loved ones if they could hold onto hope for as long as possible.

I went down to ICU with the patient, keeping an eye on the monitor as we went. I was trying not to be influenced by the air of doom and gloom that had blown up in Theatre. I had seen patients much worse than Jason recover. It was a setback, certainly, but with time and patience and careful monitoring he had a chance, maybe even better than expected, given his level of fitness.

Once Jason was settled on the ventilator I went out to the family waiting in the relatives' room. His wife, Megan, was about six months pregnant and stood with Jason's parents as soon as I came in. 'How is he?' she said, holding her hand over her belly as if to protect her baby from hearing bad news.

'The operation was very difficult, Megan,' I said in a gentle but calm tone. 'The tumour had a lot of blood running through it. Mr McTaggart was able to get it out, but not without bleeding, and there is likely a bit of damage to some of the surrounding brain. It's impossible to tell at this stage how he's going to be. There's no choice but to wait and see what effect the tumour and the operative trauma has had. But it's important to keep positive and try not to feel too overwhelmed at this stage. Everything that can be done is being done to bring about the best possible recovery for Jason.'

There was a sound behind me and I turned to see Matt Bishop come in. 'I'm sorry to keep you waiting,' he said, briefly shaking hands with Jason's parents and then Megan. 'I'm Matt Bishop, the head of ICU.'

Jason's father Ken swallowed thickly. 'What's happening to our boy?'

'He's being ventilated and kept in an induced coma,' Matt said. 'During surgery there was a major bleed from the tumour bed. Mr McTaggart was able to stop the bleed, but it's possible normal brain may have been damaged in the process. When the brain swelling has decreased, we'll gradually reduce the sedation, and see what effect the surgery has had. But I should warn you that surgery to a vascular tumour like this, and the bleeding that goes with trying to remove it, can cause a lot of damage. I'm sorry but there's a possibility he won't wake up.'

Jason's mother put a shaky hand against her throat. 'You mean he could…die?'

Matt's expression was grave. 'A bleed like the one Jason suffered can damage vital areas of the brain. In the morning we'll repeat the CT scan and try to assess what physical damage has occurred. We might be able to predict from that how he might recover. In the end, though, we just have to wait, try to wean him off sedation and see if he wakes up.'

The word lingered in the air like a toxic fume.

If, not when he wakes up.

I watched as the hope on Jason's mother's face collapsed, aging her a decade. I saw the devastation spread over Megan's, distorting her young and pretty features into a mask of horror. Jason's father's face went completely still and ashen. All their hopes and dreams for their son had been cut down with one two-letter word.

Matt answered a few more questions but it was obvious to me that the poor family weren't taking much in. They were still trying to get their heads around the fact the son and husband they had kissed that morning on his way to the operating theatre might not come back to them.

My heart ached for them. I know as a doctor you're supposed to keep a clinical distance. And I do most of the time. But now and again a patient comes along who touches you. Jason was such a normal, nice type of guy. He was exactly the same age as me. His family were loving and supportive, the sort of family who loved each other unconditionally. I thought of the baby in Megan's womb who might never get to know his or her father. I thought of the implications for Megan, trapped in a marriage to a man who might be permanently disabled, unable to talk, to eat or drink unassisted. Then there were the bathing and toileting issues—the whole heart-breaking scenario of taking care of someone who could no longer do anything for themselves. Her young life would be utterly destroyed along with his.

Once Matt left I took the family to my relaxation room where my aromatherapy infuser was releasing lavender and tangerine, which had a calming effect and was shown to be beneficial in helping with anxiety and depression. I sat with them for a few minutes, handing them tissues scented with clary sage, another stress reliever, and listened as they talked about Jason. They told me about his childhood and some funny anecdotes about him as a teenager, and of his passion for golf and how hard he worked at his game. How they had mortgaged their house and forgone holidays for years in order to sponsor his career because they believed so unreservedly in his talent.

That's the thing about busy hospitals these days. No one has time to sit with patients and their families and chat. Nurses are under the pump all the time with other patients to see to. The doctors have the pressure of clinical work and administrative duties, and in a teaching hospital such as St Iggy's the responsibility of teaching medical students, residents and interns and registrars leaves little time to linger by a patient's bedside. Often it was the cleaning or catering staff that counselled patients most, but even they were under increasing pressure.

I made a point of keeping some time for the patients, even though it meant my days were a little longer than normal. Looking back, I think that was one of the reasons Andy strayed. I just wasn't around enough for him. That, and the assumption that because my parents had an open relationship I, too, would be happy with the same arrangement. Shows how little he knew me. But he knew how much I love my work. It's not so much a career for me but a vocation. I love being able to help people and being with them through the darkest times is the most challenging but in many ways the most rewarding.

I caught up to Matt half an hour later just as he was coming out of his office. I didn't wait to be invited in. I put my hand flat on the door just as he was about to close it. 'Can I have a word?'

He drew in a breath and released it with a sound of impatience. 'I have a meeting in five minutes.'

'I'll be brief.'

He opened the door and I walked past him to enter his office. My left arm brushed against his body as I went. I brush past people all the time. It's hard not to in a busy and often crowded workplace, especially in ICU or Theatre. But I had never felt a tingle go through me quite like that before. It was like touching a bolt of lightning. Energy zapped through my entire body from my arm to my lady land. I was hoping it didn't show on my face. I'm not one to blush easily…or at least not until that morning. I stopped blushing when my parents went through their naturalist phase when I was thirteen. I think my blushing response blew a gasket back then. But right then I could feel warmth spreading in my cheeks. I could only hope he would assume it was because of the message I was there to deliver.

I got straight to the point. 'Did you have to be so blunt with Jason Ryder's wife and family? Surely you could've given them a little ray of hope? You made it sound like the poor man is going to die overnight or be a vegetable. I've seen much worse than—'

'Dr Clark.' His curt tone cut me off. 'I don't see the point in offering false hope. It's better to prepare relatives for the worst, even if it doesn't eventuate. It's much harder to do it the other way around.'

'But surely you could have dressed it up a little more—'

'You mean *lie* to them?' he said, nailing me with a look.

There was something about his stress over the word 'lie' that made my skin shrink away from my bones. I tried not to squirm under his tight scrutiny but I can tell you that hummingbird was back in my heart valve. 'I think you could have found a middle ground. They're completely shell-shocked. They need time to process everything.'

'Time is not something Jason Ryder has right now,' he said. 'That was a significant bleed. You and I both know he might not last the night.'

I pressed my lips together. I wasn't ready to give up hope, although I had to admit Jason's condition was critical.

'Have you mentioned organ donation to the family?' Matt said.

I frowned. 'No, but I'm surprised you didn't thrust the papers under their noses right then and there.'

His dark blue gaze warred with mine. 'If Jason's a registered donor then it's appropriate to get the wheels in motion as soon as possible. Other lives can be saved. The family might find it difficult at first, but further down the track it often gives comfort to know their relative's death wasn't entirely in vain.'

I knew he was right. But the subject of organ donation is enormously difficult for most people, including clinicians. Relatives are overwrought with grief, especially after an accident or a sudden illness or surgery that didn't go according to plan. They want to cling to their loved one for as long as they can, to hold them and talk to them to say their final goodbyes. Some relatives can't face the thought of their son or daughter or husband or wife being operated on to harvest organs, even when those very organs will save other lives.

It was another thing I wanted to cover in my research. Finding the right time and the right environment in which to bring up the subject could go a long way in lifting organ donation rates, which were generally abysmal. All too often organ donation directives signed by patients were reversed because the relatives were in such distress.

I let out a breath in a little whoosh. 'I'll talk to them tomorrow. I think they need tonight to come to terms with what they've been told so far.'

There was a little silence.

I was about to fill it with something banal when he said, 'Would you like Jason moved to the end room?'

I looked at him in surprise. 'But I thought—'

'It will give the family a little more privacy.'

I couldn't read his expression. He had his poker face on. 'That would be great,' I said. 'Thank you.'

He gave me the briefest of smiles. It was little more than a little quirk of his lips but it made something inside my stomach slip. I suddenly wondered what his full smile would look like and if it would have an even more devastating effect on me. 'How do you get on with Stuart McTaggart?' he said.

'Fine.'

He lifted a dark eyebrow as if that wasn't the answer he'd been expecting. 'You don't find him…difficult?'

I gave a little shrug. 'He has his moments but I don't let it get to me. He's under a lot of pressure and he doesn't know how to manage stress. Stress is contagious, like a disease. You can catch it off others if you're not careful.'

He leaned his hips back against his desk with his arms folded across his broad chest. His eyes never once left mine. I would have found it threatening except I was so fascinated by their colour I was practically mesmerised. In certain lights they were predominately grey but in others they were blue. And now and again they would develop a tiny glittery twinkle as if he was enjoying a private joke.

'So what are your top three hints for relieving stress?' he said.

'Regular exercise, eight hours' sleep, good nutrition.'

'Not so easy when you work the kind of hours we work.'

'True.'

He was still watching me with that unwavering gaze. 'What about sex?'

I felt a hot blush spread over my cheeks. Yes, I know.
I'm such a prude, which is incredibly ironic given my
parents talk about their sex lives at the drop of a sarong.
'Wh-what about it?' I stammered.

'Isn't it supposed to be the best stress-reliever of all?'

I ran the tip of my tongue out over my suddenly
parchment-dry lips. The heat in my cheeks flowed to
other parts of my body—my breasts, my belly and between my legs. Even the base of my spine felt molten
hot. 'Erm, yes, it's good for that,' I said, 'excellent, in
fact. But not everyone can have sex when they're feeling stressed. I mean, how would that work in the workplace, for instance? We can't have staff running off to
have sex in the nearest broom cupboard whenever they
feel like it, can we?'

I wished I hadn't taken the bait. I wished I hadn't
kept running off at the mouth like that. Why the hell
was I talking about sex with Matt Bishop? All I could
think of was what it would be like to have sex *with* him.
Not in a broom cupboard, although I'm sure he would
be more than up to the challenge. But in a bed with his
arms around me, his long legs entangled with mine, his
body pressing me down on the mattress in a passionate
clinch unlike any I'd had before.

Just to put you straight, I'm no untried virgin. I've
had three partners, although I don't usually count the
first one because I was drunk at the time and I can't
remember much about it. It was my first year at med
school and I was embarrassed about still being a virgin so I drank three vile-tasting cocktails at a party and
had it off with a guy whose name I still can't remember.
What is it about cocktails and me?

But I digress. The second was only slightly more memorable in that I wasn't drunk or even tipsy, but the guy had performance anxiety, so I blinked and missed it, so to speak. I guess that's why Andy had seemed such a super-stud. At least he could go the distance and I actually managed to orgasm now and again. Told you I was good at lying.

Matt kept his gaze trained on my flustered one, a hint of a smile still playing around the corners of his mouth. 'Perhaps not.'

My phone started to ring and I grabbed at it as if it were the lottery office calling to inform me of a massive win. It wasn't. It was my mother. 'Can I call you back?' I said.

'Darling, you sound so tense.' My mother's voice carried like a foghorn. I think it's from all the chanting she does. It's given her vocal cords serious muscle. 'He's not worth the angst.'

I could feel my cheeks glowing like hot embers. 'I *really* can't talk now so—'

'I just called to give you your horoscope reading. It's really amazing because it said you're going to meet—'

'Now's not a good time,' I said with a level of desperation I could barely keep out of my voice. 'I'll call you later. I promise.'

'All right, darling. Love you.' She made kissy noises.

'I love you too. Bye.' I ended the call and gave Matt a wry look. 'My mum.'

'Who's causing you the angst?' he asked. 'Not me, I hope?'

I backed my way to the door, almost tripping over

my own feet in clumsy haste. 'I'd better let you get to your meeting.'

'Dr Clark?'

My hand reached for the doorknob and I turned my head to look at him over my shoulder. 'Yes?'

A glint danced in his eyes. 'Check the broom cupboards on your way past, will you?'

CHAPTER THREE

I WAS ABOUT to leave for the day when the CEO's secretary came to see me. Lynne Patterson was in her late fifties and had worked at St Iggy's for thirty years in various administrative roles. I had only met her a handful of times but she was always warm and friendly. She reminded me of a mother hen. She oozed maternal warmth and was known for taking lame ducks under her wing. Not that I considered myself a lame duck or anything, but right then I wasn't paddling quite the way I wanted to.

'How did the wedding go?' Lynne asked as her opening gambit. *What is it with everyone and weddings?* I thought. People were becoming obsessed. It wasn't healthy.

My smile felt like it was set in plaster of Paris on my mouth. 'Great. Fabulous. Wonderful. Awesome.' I was going overboard with the superlatives but what else could I do? In for a penny, as they say, but now I was in for a million. I had to keep telling lies to keep the others in place. I was starting to realise what a farce this was becoming. I would have been better to be honest from the start. But now it was too late. I would look completely ridiculous if I told everyone the wedding had been cancelled. Maybe in a couple of months I could say things didn't work out, that Andy and I had decided to separate or something. But until then I had to keep the charade going. *Oh, joy.*

'Well, that's why I thought you'd be perfect for the job,' Lynne said with a beaming smile.

'Erm…job?'

'The St Valentine's Day Ball,' she said. 'We hold it every year. It's our biggest fundraising event for the hospital. But this year it's ICU that's going to get the funds we raise. We hope to raise enough for an intensive care training simulator.'

I'd heard about the ball but I thought it was being organised by one of the senior paediatricians. I said as much but Lynne explained the consultant had to go on leave due to illness so they needed someone to take over.

'Besides,' Lynne said, 'you're young and hip and in touch with everything. The ball was becoming a little staid and boring. Ticket sales have been slow. We thought you'd be fabulous at putting on a great party.'

'We?'

'Dr Bishop.' Lynne beamed again. 'He said you'd be perfect.'

I did the teeth-grinding thing. Silently, I hoped, but I wouldn't have put money on it. 'Right, well, then, I guess I can do that,' I said, madly panicking because it was barely four weeks away. I comforted myself with the fact I didn't have to organise the venue or catering as the consultant had already done that, according to Lynne. My job was to make the ball entertaining and fun for everyone.

As soon as I got out of the hospital I called Jem. She's a teacher—another irony, given our parents went through a no-schooling phase. It lasted three years but then the authorities cottoned on and we were marched back into the system. Interestingly, I was a year ahead of my peers academically but well behind socially. For Jem it was the other way around. She had no trouble fitting in but she struggled to catch up in classwork. She's never said, but I'm pretty sure that's why she ended up a teacher. She understands how hard it is for kids who aren't naturally academic. Mind you, she's no dunce. Once she caught up there was no stopping her. She whizzed her way through university, landing the vice chancellor's prize on the way through. Now she teaches at a posh girls' school in Bath.

'Jem, you got a minute to talk?' I asked.

'Sure,' Jem said. 'What's up? I mean, apart from being betrayed by your fiancé with the slutty sister of your bridesmaid, and then jilted at the altar, and going on honeymoon all by yourself.'

That's another reason I love my sister. She doesn't sugar-coat stuff. She doesn't just take the bull by the horns. She wrenches the darned things off. Unlike me, who tentatively pets the bull in the hope it will become my best friend and won't gore me to death. But one thing Jem and I have in common is a love of black humour. It's how we dealt with our wacky childhood. If we hadn't laughed we'd have cried. 'It's way worse than that,' I said, and told her about the postcard fiasco.

'What? You mean you still haven't told anyone? No one at all?'

'No.' I kept my head down against the icy cold wind

as I walked along the frozen footpath. The last thing I wanted was to slip and end up in the orthopaedic ward. Although come to think of it…

'What about your friend, what's her name? The nurse you said was really sweet.'

'Gracie.'

'That's the one. What about her?'

I sidestepped a sheet of black ice. I decided I didn't want to break a leg. How would I explain no husband coming in to visit me? 'I'm going to tell her…soon.'

'It's not that hard, Bertie,' Jem said matter-of-factly. 'You have nothing to be ashamed of. Andy's a twat. You don't have to protect him. Tell the world what a flipping jerk he is.'

I guess you can tell by now Jem is not the sort of girl to get screwed around by guys. In fact, I think she terrifies most men, which kind of explains why she hasn't had a steady boyfriend for ages—years, actually. She dated a Sicilian guy once but it didn't last. It was a whirlwind affair that ended badly. She's never talked about it. Won't talk about it. I know better than to ask.

'I got caught off guard because of the new director at work,' I said. 'It was too embarrassing to go into the gory details.' *Understatement.*

'What's he like?'

'How do you know he's a he?'

'Because you wouldn't have been caught off guard if it was a woman.'

Got to hand it to my sister. She knows me so well. 'He's…annoying, but kind of interesting too.'

'Woo hoo!' Jem crowed.

I rolled my eyes. I knew what she was thinking—the

best way to heal a broken heart was to find someone
else and soon. But I'd had enough trouble finding Andy.
I didn't like my chances in the dating game. Besides,
I'm not sure I wanted all the drama. Maybe I was des-
tined to be on my own. My heart sank at the thought.
I didn't want to be alone. I wanted to be with someone
who loved me. I wanted a family. I wanted it all. 'He
thinks my research is dodgy,' I said.

'What's he look like?'

'Did you hear me?' I said.

'Is he hot?'

'He's okay.'

'How okay?' Jem said.

I blew out a breath. There was no point fighting it.
Jem would get it out of me eventually. Might as well be
sooner rather than later. 'He's six foot four and has dark
hair and blue-grey eyes that change in different lights.
He's got a nice mouth but I don't think he smiles at lot.
Although he gets this little twinkle now and again that
makes me wonder if he's laughing at me.'

'Way to go, Bertie!'

'Like that's going to happen,' I said. 'Besides, he
thinks I'm married.'

'Some men get off on having an affair with a married woman.'

'Not him,' I said. 'He's too conservative.' Which was
kind of what I liked about him, even though I was supposed to dislike him on account of him being so mocking about my project. But for all that I felt drawn to him.
He intrigued me. All those shifting shadows in his eyes
suggested a man with layers and secrets that were just
waiting to be explored.

'So what doesn't he like about your research?' Jem asked. 'Apart from the funny title, of course.'

I almost tripped on a crack in the footpath. 'Why didn't you say something earlier?'

Jem laughed. 'I thought you did it deliberately. You know how everyone is always poking fun at New Agey things. I thought it was really clever of you, actually.'

'Yeah, well, Matt Bishop thinks it's a big joke,' I said. 'It will be all round the hospital tomorrow. I just know it. Everyone will be laughing at me.'

'You've been laughed at before and lived to tell the tale,' Jem said. 'We both have.'

I couldn't argue with that. Sometimes when I couldn't sleep I heard the mocking taunts from my childhood echoing in my bedroom. They were like ghosts from the past who wouldn't leave me alone. Mean ghosts who delighted in reminding me I wasn't part of the in-crowd. I was a misfit. A reject. A loner. Alone.

I said goodbye to Jem and walked through the park to my house a couple of streets back from Bayswater Road. I was really proud of my home. I had a shockingly high mortgage, which would take me the rest of my life to pay off, but I didn't care. I loved my three-storey Victorian house with its quaint pocket-handkerchief front garden.

I was teaching myself how to paint and decorate, not just to save costs but because I found it therapeutic. There was something incredibly soothing about painting. I was doing a room at a time and really enjoyed seeing the transformation happen before my eyes. Cracked and peeling paint replaced by smooth fresh colour. I'd done the master bedroom and now I was working on the sitting room. I scrubbed and sanded back the woodwork and applied the first undercoat before I left for my… well, you know. Andy was going to help me finish it. Or at least that's what he'd said. Not that he'd helped me with any of it, although I do seem to remember once he carried some old wallpaper out to the recycling bin.

My dad isn't much help. He can barely change a light bulb, mostly because he and Mum went through a no-electricity phase, which lasted about ten years. Solar power is great when you live in a place like Australia where the sun shines just about every day. Not so good on the Yorkshire moors.

I had a bite to eat and set to work but I had barely got the undercoat lid off the paint tin when there was a knock on the door. I peeped through the spy hole. It was the neighbour who lives six houses up from Elsie. Margery Stoneham was in her mid-seventies and was our street's neighbourhood watch. Nothing escaped her notice. She had an annoying yappy little dog called Freddy who humped my leg any chance it got. Don't get me wrong. I love animals, dogs in particular, but Freddy was the most obnoxious little mutt I'd ever come across. He looked like a cross between a ferret and a rat and had the sort of wiry fur that felt like a pot scourer.

I felt on the back foot as soon as I opened the door. I had—inadvertently—sent Margery a postcard, along with Elsie. Who could believe three little pieces of cardboard could do so much damage? The dog was at Margery's feet, looking up at me with a beady look not unlike hers. 'Hi, Mrs Stoneham,' I said, with a bright smile. 'What a lovely surprise.' *Not.*

Margery peered past my shoulder. 'Is your hubby at home?'

'Erm, not right now.' *Here we go again*, I thought. But Margery was the last person I wanted to announce my failed wedding to. I might as well take out a billboard ad or announce it in *The Times*. 'How's that leg ulcer? Healed up now?' Freddy had taken a nip at her, not that she admitted that to me. She told me she'd scratched it on the coffee table. I checked out the coffee table when I was over there, dressing the wound for her. As far as I could tell it didn't have any teeth.

'Just about.' Margery looked past my shoulder again. 'Are you sure I'm not intruding? You're only just back from your honeymoon. I wouldn't want to—'

'It's perfectly fine,' I said. 'What can I do for you?'

That's one thing I did know for sure. Margery nearly always wanted something. She didn't just drop in for a chat. I can't tell you how many prescriptions I've written for her and I've only been living there just under a year.

'I wanted to ask a little favour of you,' she said. 'I'm going to visit my sister in Cornwall and I need someone to mind Freddy for a few days. I'd ask Elsie but she's not confident walking him and he does so love his walk.'

I wanted to say no. Jem would have said no but, then, she's a lot stronger than I am. I have this annoying tendency to want to please everyone. I say yes when I really want to say no because I'm worried people won't like me if I grow a backbone. 'Of course I'll mind him,' I said. See how good I am at lying? They just slip off my tongue. 'We'll have a ball, won't we, Freddy?'

I knew better than to lean down and try and pat him. He lifted one side of his mouth in a snarl that showed his yellowed teeth. Did I mention his foetid breath? Oh, and he farts. A lot.

* * *

When I got to work the next morning there was no change in Jason Ryder. He had been moved to my end room and was surrounded by his family. I spent a bit of time with them before I did a central line on a new patient. The morning was almost over before I ran into Matt Bishop. Literally. I was walking past his office with my head down, thinking about my ridiculous and steadily increasing web of lies, as he was coming out, and I cannoned straight into him. He took me by the upper arms to steady me and a shockwave went through me as if he had clamped me with live voltage. I couldn't smother a gasp in time. 'Oomph!'

His hands slid down my arms before he released me. I couldn't help noticing he opened and closed his fingers once or twice as if trying to rid himself of the feel of me. 'Sorry. Did I hurt you?'

I looked into his eyes—they were a darker shade of blue than grey as he was wearing a light blue shirt and a dark tie—and I felt like something tight and locked flowered open inside my chest. 'No. Not at all. It was my fault. I wasn't looking where I was going.'

He continued to look down at me. He had to look down as I'm only five feet five and I wasn't wearing heels. I felt like a Shetland pony standing in front of a thoroughbred. And, going with the equine theme, Matt's nostrils gave a slight flare, as if he was picking up my scent. I hoped to God it was the dash of the neroli oil I'd put on and not the musty smell of Freddy, who'd been dropped off that morning. 'Did Lynne Patterson speak to you about the ball?' he said.

'Yes. Thanks for the vote of confidence.' I couldn't quite remove the hint of sarcasm from my tone. 'I hope you don't live to regret it.'

'I'm sure you'll do an excellent job.' He gave me one of his enigmatic smiles. 'Planning a wedding can't be too dissimilar.'

Every time the word 'wedding' was mentioned I felt my cheeks burn up. I was going to have to wear thick concealing make-up or something at this rate. Or maybe I could pretend I had rosacea. 'I'm going to check out the venue after work,' I said. 'And I'm thinking we should make it a costume ball. What do you think?'

'That could work.'

I angled my head at him. 'What costume would you wear?'

The twinkle was back in his gaze. 'Now, that would be telling. You'll have to wait and see.'

'Will you bring a partner?' I'm not sure why I asked that. Actually, I did know. I wanted to know what sort of woman he dated. I bet he would be a wonderful partner. He would be polite and respectful. He would open doors for his date and walk on the road side of the footpath. I bet he could dance, too, proper dancing as in a waltz. Andy mashed my toes to a pulp on the one occasion we waltzed. And he got horribly drunk and I had to get two security guards to help me bundle him into a taxi. Talk about embarrassing.

'No.'

'Why not? Surely you could ask someone.'

He gave a loose shrug. 'I'm too busy for a relationship just now. I have other priorities.' He waited a beat before asking, 'Will you bring your husband?'

He'd done it again, that ever so slight stress on the word 'husband'. Every time he did that it made me feel as if he thought I was too hideous to have landed myself a man. I know I'm not billboard stunning or anything but I've been told I've got nice brown eyes and a cute smile. Well, I know parents are always biased, but still. 'Erm, I think he'll be away with work,' I said. 'He travels…a lot.'

'That's a shame. I was looking forward to meeting him.'

I wrinkled my brow. 'Why?'

His expression was impossible to read. 'You said he was a stock analyst, right?'

'Yes…'

'I thought I'd ask him about some stocks I've had my eye on for a while.'

I shifted my weight from foot to foot. I felt a heat rash moving all over my body. It was like ants marching underneath my skin. Maybe my talent at lying was deserting me. 'Don't you have a financial planner?' I said.

'Sure, but it's always good to get inside information, don't you think?'

I couldn't hold his penetrating gaze. I lowered mine and mumbled something about seeing a patient and left.

I was walking Freddy in Hyde Park in one of the dog exercise areas after work. It was freezing cold and flakes of snow were falling but I was determined to wear out the little mutt. While I'd been at work he'd chewed my favourite hippopotamus slippers Jem gave me for Christmas two years ago and one of my computer cables. I decided to let him off the lead so he could have a good run around and play with the other dogs. What I hadn't realised was that Freddy didn't *like* other dogs. Before I knew it he was at the throat of a corgi and it looked like Freddy was winning. The howls and growls and yelps and cries of 'Help!' from me created such a ruckus that people did what people normally do in that situation—they stopped and stared and did absolutely nothing.

Except for one man who came out of the shadows and pulled the dogs apart with his bare hands. Except his hands weren't bare. He was wearing gloves, lovely butter-soft black leather ones that Freddy's teeth immediately punctured. I grabbed Freddy and snapped his lead back on but the stupid mutt was straining at the leash, trying to get to the overweight corgi, who was doing the same on the end of its lead, which its owner had now refastened.

'I'm *so* sorry,' I said. 'It's not my dog. I didn't realise he would...' I blinked as the man's face was suddenly illuminated by one of the park's lights. 'You!'

Matt Bishop gave me a rueful look. 'It's not my dog either. It's my great-aunt's.'

'Your great-aunt isn't the Queen, is she?'

He threw back his head and laughed. I stood transfixed at the sound. It was deep and unmistakably masculine and made something deep and tight in my belly work loose. It wasn't just his laugh that was so captivating. It was the way his normally stern features relaxed, giving him an almost boyish look. At work with the pressures of lives in his hands he looked as if he was nudging forty. Now he looked no older than thirty but I knew he had to be at least thirty-three or -four to be as qualified as he was to head the department.

He was wearing casual clothes under a dark blue cashmere overcoat. Jeans and a sweater with the tips of his shirt collar showing. I don't think I've ever seen a more handsome-looking man. Not in a pretty-boy way but in a totally testosterone-oozing way that made the breath catch in my throat.

His gaze went to the cup-cake beanie I was wearing. It was pink and white and had a red pom-pom on top that looked like a cherry. I was pretty proud of it, actually. I taught myself to knit, making novelty beanies. So far I've made a mouse, a zebra and a bee.

The dogs were still snarling at each other. I had Freddy on such a tight leash I could feel the muscles in my arm protesting at the strain. Who needed the gym when you had an unruly dog? Freddy hurt more than three sets of ten-kilogram biceps curls.

'Quiet, Winnie,' Matt said. The corgi slunk down into a submissive pose but not before giving Freddy another murderous look. Freddy growled like something out of a horror movie and completely ignored my command to be quiet. I guess because my voice wasn't as deep and authoritative as Matt's, because as soon as Matt said it to Freddy he sat and shut up. He even held up his paw for a shake.

'Nice job,' I said. 'You don't happen to be best friends with Cesar Millan, do you?'

Matt smiled and my breath caught again. 'Dog training's pretty simple. You just have to show them who's pack leader.'

I'm not sure how it happened but somehow we started walking together. The dogs kept eyeing each other warily, but after a while they seemed to forget their ignominious start and got on with the job of sniffing every blade of grass…well, the ones that weren't covered in snow, that is. A light dusting had fallen, making the park look like a winter fairyland. I love winter. I think it's the most romantic time of the year. That's why I wanted to be married in early December. Everyone gets married in spring or summer. I wanted to be different. But, then, sometimes you can be too different, which I've found to my detriment.

'Where does your great-aunt live?' I asked into the silence. Actually, I was quite proud of the fact I'd waited at least thirty seconds before speaking. That's a record for me.

He named the street running parallel to mine. I was so shocked I stopped and looked up at him. 'Really?'

'What's wrong?' he asked.

I gave a shaky laugh. 'Whoa, that's spooky. I live in the next street. Number forty.'

'Why spooky?'

'As in weirdly coincidental,' I said. 'London's a big city.'

'True, but it's close to the hospital and I'm only staying there until I can move back into my place once the tenants move out in a couple of weeks.'

He was living a street away from me?

'Where is your place?'

'Notting Hill.'

Of course, I thought. I'd had a feeling Matt came from money. He had the right accent and the well-groomed and cultured look. It had taken me years to shake off my Yorkshire vowels. Now and again when I was overtired one would slip out. I privately envied people like Matt. They hadn't been dragged around the countryside in search of the next New Age trend, living in mud huts or tents or straw houses, not eating animal products or wearing them, not using chemicals or eating sugar or salt or processed food.

Don't get me wrong. I love my parents. They're good people, loving and kind and well meaning. But I couldn't imagine Matt Bishop's parents cavorting around a stone circle stark naked and chanting mantras. They probably wore Burberry and sipped sherry in the conservatory of their centuries-old pile in the countryside while a host of servants tended to their every whim.

'How long have you got the dog?' Matt asked.

'Until the weekend after next,' I said. 'My neighbour is visiting her sister in Cornwall. I don't know why she didn't take him with her. Maybe her sister won't let her. Can't say I blame her. He needs to go to reform school.'

I heard him give a soft, deep chuckle and another shiver shimmied down my spine.

'My great-aunt is visiting my parents for a few days,' he said.

I cast him a sideways glance. 'Your parents don't like dogs?'

Nothing showed on his face but the tone of his voice contained a hint of something I couldn't identify. 'My father.'

'Is he allergic?'

His mouth tightened for a nanosecond. 'You could say that.'

'Do you have siblings?' I asked, after we'd walked a few more paces. See how good I was getting at silences? Maybe there was some hope for me after all.

'No,' he said after a slight pause. 'There's only me. You?'

'A sister called Jem—short for Jemima. Our mum was really into Beatrix Potter, in case you hadn't guessed. Jem's ten months older than me.'

He flashed me a quick glance. 'That was close.'

I rolled my eyes. 'My parents were using natural contraceptive methods. So natural they fell pregnant straight away.'

He smiled again. 'Are you close to your sister?'

'Very, although we're quite different.'

'What does she do?'

'She's a teacher.'

We walked a few more metres in silence. Yes, in silence! But for some reason I didn't feel awkward or pressured to fill it. I wondered about his parents, whether he was close to them or not. I sensed tension between him and his father but that might just be my imagination. Although a lot of men of Matt's age had the young stag, old stag thing going on. It could be quite a competitive dynamic, especially as the father neared retirement age.

'What does your father do?' I asked.

'He's in corporate law.'

'Does your mother have a career?'

'She used to work as a legal secretary but she didn't

go back after she married.' He waited a beat before adding, 'My father likes having her at his beck and call.'

I frowned at his tone. 'Is that what *she* wants?'

He shrugged the shoulder nearest me. I felt it brush against mine. 'She seems happy enough being the trophy wife. It's either that or get traded in for a newer model. At least he's spared her the indignity of that.'

I was surprised—and secretly delighted—he'd revealed that to me. I wondered if he felt I was someone he could talk to about stuff. It's hard for doctors, particularly specialists at the top of their field. Everyone comes to *them* to solve their problems. No one ever thinks to ask if the specialist has problems of his or her own. I suspected Matt had some frustration towards his mother for settling for a life of sherry mornings and bridge club. Did his father play around? Openly or furtively?

I thought of my parents with their easygoing lifestyle. They loved each other. No one could ever be in doubt of that, least of all Jem and I. They were open about their—thankfully occasional these days—other partners, which Jem and I still found totally weird, but they always came back to each other and would never dream of stopping each other from reaching their potential. If my mum wanted to do something, my dad would support her in it one hundred percent, and vice versa. They didn't have secrets, or at least none Jem and I were aware of.

I decided against telling Matt about my background. He didn't ask, which either meant he wasn't interested or he was tired of small talk. Or maybe he regretted revealing what he had. I glanced at him covertly to find he had a frown on his forehead.

The dogs were walking to heel like star graduates from obedience school. I felt a little proud of myself, actually. Maybe I could win over Freddy by the time Margery got back. Have him eating out of my hand instead of biting it.

'Have you checked out the venue for the ball?' Matt asked.

'No, I thought I'd do that once I wore out Freddy.'

He stopped and looked down at me. I couldn't see his eyes because his face was in shadow but I could see the misty fog of his warm breath as it met the cold air. 'How about I come with you? That is, if your husband wouldn't mind?'

My heart gave a little stumble as I gave him one of my fixed smiles. 'Believe me, he won't mind at all.'

CHAPTER FOUR

MATT CAME TO pick me up in his car forty-five minutes later. I'd had just enough time to feed Freddy and wash his musty wet feathers smell off me. I spritzed myself with my neroli oil spray and brushed out my hair, which had been in a knot at the back of my head for work and then squashed flat by my beanie.

I'm not in the least bit vain but I will say one thing for myself—I have great hair. It's thick and healthy with just enough wave in it to give it loads of body, or I can straighten it, and it's long enough to put up or leave loose. Jem hates me for it, as hers is a riot of corkscrew blonde curls that makes her look like she's poked her fingers into a power outlet.

I was waiting on my front step as Matt's car double-parked. There are never any spaces in front of my house, which is usually my biggest bugbear, but tonight I was glad about it. The last thing I wanted was for Matt Bishop to park his car outside my door and invite himself in. One step inside and my charade would be blown. There wasn't a single thing to suggest I was a recently married woman, and it wasn't just the absence of a husband either. I had sent back all the wedding gifts…

apart from the really gorgeous art deco standard lamp Jem had given me.

Before I'd taken a step off my front porch Matt got out of the car and opened the passenger door for me. His gaze ran over my hair and my outfit in a way that made me feel as if he was seeing me for the first time. I actually saw him blink a couple of times as if he couldn't believe what he was seeing. I had changed into a raspberry-red knee-length dress and I'd teamed it with black leather boots—I tell my parents they're synthetic—and I was wearing fishnet tights. I was wearing a fake-fur coat— even *I* am with my parents on that—but I have to admit there was a hint of high-street hooker about my get-up. But, then, I love playful clothes. Not just so people will laugh at them instead of me, but more to put my finger up at the world for making snap judgements about appearances. We are all the same naked…well, more or less.

Mind you, I was having hot flushes thinking about Matt Bishop in his birthday suit. Even though he had a tall, rangy build, his neat, conservative clothes weren't quite able to hide the firm tone of his muscles. I could imagine how taut and toned his abdomen was, unlike mine, which was paying the price of a two-week stint of comfort eating.

I slipped into the low-slung sports car, the rich, soft leather seat cupping my body like an expensively gloved hand. I could smell Matt's subtle aftershave and took a deep breath to take more of it in as I pulled down the seat belt and clicked it into place.

He got in behind the wheel and I covertly watched the muscles bunching in his thigh as he put his foot down on the clutch and put the car into gear. There's something about a manual car that's intensely masculine. Surging through all those gears, the guttural sound of all those throaty revs, the G-force as the rubber hits the road. I felt myself being pushed back further into the seat as we headed to the corner.

The hotel where the hospital ball was being held was a boutique one owned by a former patient. We were getting the use of the ballroom at a cut price. The hotel was popular with A-list celebrities because it was both intimate and luxurious. I hadn't been there before so I felt like a Hollywood superstar walking up the runner of red carpet on the front steps leading into the polished marble foyer. Uniformed staff were behind the shiny brass and marble reception desk and there was a concierge and three porters in another section. There was a massive arrangement of flowers on a marble stand and a veritable waterfall of crystals hung from the ceiling in a gloriously decadent chandelier that tinkled musically as we walked under it.

I didn't want to appear too kid-in-the-candy-store overwhelmed by all the glitz and glamour surrounding me, but given I hadn't stepped into a proper hotel until I was eighteen I still had a lot of catching up to do. My parents didn't even stay in motels or caravan parks, let alone posh five-star hotels. They camped. And before you start picturing a nicely erected tent and a crackling fire and us four sitting around it singing 'Kumbaya', let me tell you it was nothing like that. We didn't have a proper tent. My parents always borrowed one that looked like it had a past life in the circus. It was huge. But that was because there were usually ten other families with us, which meant Jem and I had to hang out with a bunch of feral kids we had nothing in common with apart from having hippy parents.

It nearly always rained, and we were bitten to death by midges, or it was stinking hot and ants would get in our food, which was ironic given there was never any sugar in it.

So you can probably see why walking into the boutique hotel in Mayfair was such a big deal for me. Oh, and the fact that I was walking in with Matt Bishop was even more thrilling. We were getting looks. You know, the sort of double-take looks people give when they think they're seeing someone important walk by.

I can tell you, I *felt* important. I only wished I really was with Matt, I wished his hand was holding mine or his arm was around my waist. I was a little shocked at where my thoughts were straying. I hoped he couldn't read my mind. It was hard enough keeping my body language under control.

Matt had had the foresight to call the hotel ahead of time and make an appointment to see the ballroom. Typical me, I was just going to wing it, pop my head through the door and see what it was like. But, no, he had organised a guided tour.

The staff member left us in the ballroom while he took a call. Luckily for us the ballroom wasn't being used. The chairs and tables were against the walls, which made the floor space seem the size of a football field. The décor was a stylishly neutral one in cream and white with a touch of taupe, which gave wonderful scope for thematic decorations.

I did a three-sixty about the room and pictured stunning colours and costumes and wonderful food and wine and fabulous music with live musicians playing. I momentarily forgot about the hospital budget, but still...

'What do you think?' Matt said from beside me.

'It's perfect,' I said. 'We could have helium balloon trees and a chocolate fountain and a prize for the best costume.'

'Sounds like a plan.'

I was about to respond when the hotel staff member returned. He had an apologetic look on his face as he handed Matt a key card. 'I'm afraid I've been called away to deal with a little matter in Reception. The manager asked me to give you access to our honeymoon suite. It's the only suite that's vacant this evening so you won't be disturbed. A light supper will be sent up shortly, compliments of the hotel.'

'Oh, but we couldn't possibly—' I began.

'That's very kind,' Matt said, smiling at the staff member.

The honeymoon suite?

As we made our way to the lift my heart was skipping all around my chest cavity like a hyperactive kid on a pogo stick. I didn't say a word as the lift zoomed up to the top floor. Not one word. I did what most people do in lifts. I stared at the numbers, then at my feet, then at the 'In Case of Emergency' instructions, which I studiously memorised. Anywhere but at the tall, silent man standing within arm's reach of me. I kept my arms close to my body, clutching my purse across my belly, which was doing a series of super-fast somersaults that would have made an Olympic gymnast proud.

The lift opened and Matt led the way to the suite down the wide, velvet-soft carpeted corridor, holding the door open for me once he'd unlocked it. 'I feel as if I should be carrying you over the threshold or something,' he said with a deadpan expression.

I gave him a wry look. 'The last time someone carried me they herniated a disc.'

It was true. My dad picked me up as a joke a few years ago and ended up having months of physiotherapy. Not that I'm a big girl or anything but ever since then I've been self-conscious about my weight. It doesn't help that my father keeps reminding me of it every time he sees me by leaning over and groaning, 'My poor old aching back!'

Matt closed the door, looking at me with one of those quirked-brow looks. 'Not your husband, surely?'

I had to work hard to get myself together. 'Erm...no. He didn't carry me over the threshold. He's not very... erm...traditional.'

'Is that why you don't wear an engagement and wedding ring?'

I mentally kicked myself. I never wear rings of any sort at work because it's all too easy to lose them when I scrub up for a central line procedure or Theatre. But I should have thought of wearing a dress ring or something tonight. I'd given back Andy's engagement ring... after I'd got the plumber to find it in the S bend of my bathroom basin. I curled my fingers into my palm—as if that was going to help—and gave Matt a tight smile. 'I forgot to put them on when I got home from work. Silly me.' I spun round to look at the suite rather than have him study me in that penetrating way. 'Wow! Look at this place. It's totally awesome.'

I wasn't exaggerating. It *was* awesome. The suite

was in four compartments separated by different levels. The décor was lavishly decadent, lots of velvet and satin, with soft lighting creating a sensual mood. The sitting-room area overlooked the Thames with views over Tower Bridge and the brightly lit London Eye. A wide flat-screen television dominated one wall. Seriously, who needed a television while on honeymoon? Mind you, I was glad I had one on mine but that's because, well, you know, but at least I'd caught up on the complete box set of *Downton Abbey*. There was a well-stocked bar and a coffee table and side tables with gorgeous lamps that created an intimate atmosphere.

I caught a glimpse of the bathroom through the open door. It was bigger than my sitting room and was a luxurious affair of marble and gold with a white claw-foot bath in the centre of the room. A shower stall big enough for a hockey match was on one side and twin basins and gilt-framed mirrors above them on the other. Gorgeous fluffy towels, which looked as big as sheets, were on the gold towel rails or folded on a gold luggage rack-style holder.

On the top level of the suite there was a king-sized bed. I wondered if there was such a thing as emperor-sized—or maybe dictator-sized—as I'd never seen one as big as that before. The bedhead and sashed curtains either side of it were plush scarlet velvet, and teamed with the snow-white linen it looked not just stunning but temptingly inviting. I wasn't tired but I had a childish desire to bounce up and down on that big bed, like Jem and I used to do when we visited our grandparents, which was rare because our parents hadn't wanted us to be corrupted by capitalist greed. Like *that* worked.

There were dried rose petals artfully arranged on the bed and scatter cushions in the same rich scarlet were positioned against the bank of feather pillows. The bedside tables held twin lamps with sparkling crystal stands and the shades were the same pure white as the bed linen.

I stole a glance at Matt but he seemed totally unfazed by all the luxury. I suspected he was no stranger to five-star hotels. He was checking his phone, scrolling through messages or emails. 'Nice view,' I said to break the silence.

He looked up and smiled a lazy half-smile. 'Yes.'

I could feel my face blushing like the colour of a stoplight. Something about his gaze as it held mine made me feel like a teenager discovering she was attractive to the opposite sex for the first time. I felt aware of my body in a way I hadn't been before, all of its secret zones lighting up like a Christmas tree. Not just lighting up but fizzing with energy. I moistened my lips and watched as his gaze followed the pathway of my tongue. I saw his eyes darken as they came back to mine.

A knock on the door jolted me out of the moment. I whipped around and opened it before Matt could take a step. I knew I was acting like a gauche fool but I had never been so far out of my depth.

A hotel staff member wheeled in a trolley full of silver dome-covered dishes. There was a bottle of champagne in an ice bucket and two crystal flutes. The champagne had a scarlet ribbon tied around its neck the same shade as the cushions and drapes. I felt like I had stepped into a fairytale. I was suddenly a princess being served in the royal suite with a handsome suitor.

The handsome suitor discreetly tipped the hotel staff member and the door closed with a soft little click that had a hint of finality to it that was strangely disquieting. For some reason an anticipatory shiver coursed over my flesh. I sensed we had crossed a threshold, one I hadn't crossed in a long time. Maybe ever.

I was alone with a man I had only met the day before.

He was my boss, sure, but if things had been different—like if I weren't pretending to be married—I would have been perfectly happy if we were left alone for the next week. Month even.

'Might as well make the most of the situation,' Matt said, as he reached for the champagne bottle.

I watched as he poured the bubbles into the two glasses. My fingers brushed against his as he handed me my glass. My heart fluttered and thumped like it had developed wings and a limp. My pulse raced. I took a sip…more than a sip, to be honest. It's why I don't drink too often. If I'm feeling nervous I drink more than I should.

Before I knew it the glass was empty. I could feel the alcohol hit my bloodstream like rocket fuel. I felt light-headed but maybe that had more to do with the fact that Matt was standing close enough for me to hear him breathing. I could smell those grace notes of lemongrass and lime. I could see the shadow of stubble on his jaw, so dark and so sexy I wanted to trail my fingertips across it to see if they would catch like silk does on something rough.

He put his glass down after only taking a sip. I saw his eyes move between each of mine, back and forth, and then his gaze dipped to my mouth. I stopped breathing as his head came down as if in slow motion.

I know I should have stepped away. All it would have taken was half a step. But my feet were glued in place. Bolted to the floor. I lowered my lashes as his warm breath danced over my lips. I'm not sure how long we stood there like that, with our breaths mingling so intimately. It felt like no time at all and yet it felt like forever. I ached for him to close the distance. Every cell in my body was throbbing in eagerness. I could feel the entire surface of my lips tingling for his final touchdown.

And then it happened.

I'm not sure which one of us moved first but suddenly his mouth brushed mine, a feather-light touch that triggered a seismic reaction in every nerve in my lips. I felt them tingle and fizz as his mouth came back for more, harder this time, an increase in pressure that made my heart bang against my breastbone like a church bell pulled by a madman. His lips were warm and dry and firm and commanding. They were hard and then they were soft, tempting and then teasing. I stepped up on tiptoe, my breasts pushing against the hard wall of his chest; at the same time one of his hands settled in the small of my back and brought me closer.

I felt the outline of his body from chest to thigh. It was imprinted on my flesh, setting off spot fires everywhere we touched. My breasts swelled and ached and my nipples tightened. My belly quivered against the ridged plane of his. My pelvis throbbed as I felt the length and potency of his growing erection.

I hummed with pleasure against his lips, and then

he deepened the kiss with a bold sweep and thrust of his tongue into my mouth. The sensation of our tongues meeting was like an eruption. I leaned into him, into his kiss as if it was my only source of sustenance. I tasted the hint of champagne he had sipped, but it was the mint and maleness of him that was even more addictive.

I took succour at his mouth, letting my tongue wrangle with his in a catch-me-if-you-can game that made my spine shiver in reaction. Fireworks went off in my head. My brain was so jazzed by the sensations I was feeling it was like being short-circuited. Thoughts and rationality were pushed aside as lust and need took over. I had never had a kiss so exciting, so utterly captivating I forgot all sense of time and place. I was swept up in the moment of rapture, of feeling desired and desirable, of feeling feminine and powerful in a way I had never experienced before.

His hands were suddenly cupping my face, his fingers splayed across my cheeks as he savoured my mouth as if it were his last meal. The desire that arced and burned between us took me by surprise. I had a feeling it took him by surprise too. I felt it in the way he groaned as his tongue tangled with mine, the way his body ground against mine in that primal search for satisfaction. I could feel the potency of him against my belly, the blood surging in him, extending him. Hardening him.

My own body was in raptures of excitement. I could feel lust blasting through me like dynamite blasts through shale. My inner core quivered, moistened, swelled and ached. My breasts felt fuller and more sensitive where the wall of his chest was abrading them. My lips were swelling under the mounting pressure of his mouth, my tongue fizzy with delight as it danced with his. He took my lower lip in his teeth in a soft little play-bite that made every hair on my scalp shiver at the roots. Then he swept his tongue over the spot he'd nipped, salving it, teasing it into wanting more.

I nipped at his lip, taking the flesh between my teeth and gently tugging, my insides shuddering with pleasure as he made a guttural sound of approval. I went at him again, not just his lip this time but his neck as well. I practically turned into a vampire. I sank my teeth into his skin and sucked and sucked. I probably would have drawn blood but for the fact he took me by the hair at the back of my head to control me.

But I didn't want to be controlled. Something inside me had got out of its cage. It was on a rampage. It was hurtling through every boundary or barrier I had put up in the past. My wild woman was on the loose. She was wanton and shameless and hot for action.

I went for his mouth again, crushing my lips to his, searching for his tongue with a brazen stroke of mine. He was ready and waiting for me. It was hard to tell who was more in control or if we both were on some crazy out-of-character roller-coaster ride of wild animal-driven lust.

His hands were at my breasts, shaping them through my clothes as his mouth kept up its passionate assault on mine. The feel of his hands cupping me was so wickedly delightful. It didn't matter that three layers separated his flesh from mine. I felt his touch as if he had stripped me stark naked.

I wasn't letting him cop a feel unless I got one too. I put my hands on him through his trousers, shaping him, teasing him with the bold stroke of my fingers. He was so hard I could feel the blood pounding through him. And he was getting harder. That thrilled me more than anything. There's nothing more of a turn-on than feeling a man's ardent desire for you. It made my desire flare like fuel exposed to a naked flame. I practically exploded with a fireball of lust that shook me to the centre of my being.

Every part of my body quaked with need, with longing so primal and so intense I felt like a stranger to myself. I realised then how lacklustre Andy had been. He had never touched me through my clothes as if he was too impatient to take them off before he had me. He had never growled and groaned against my mouth as if he was imbibing a potent drug and it was the only thing keeping him alive. He had never made me feel as if I was the only woman who could bring him undone with just a kiss.

I should *not* have thought of Andy. Talk about taking a cold shower. It was like a bucket of ice water had been dumped down the back of my dress.

What was I doing?

I pulled back from Matt as if he had suddenly turned to fire. 'What do you think you're doing?' I said, acting like an outraged virgin in a Regency novel. I know it was a little late for such histrionics but I had to make up some lost ground. What sort of woman did he think I was? Or was he the type who got off on dallying with married women? I had met plenty of men like that. They disgusted me. They had no sense of loyalty. No sense of the damage they were causing.

His expression was unmistakably mocking. 'What's wrong?'

'What's wrong?' I all but spluttered the words at him. 'You know exactly what's wrong! This is wrong. Us kissing like this. It's tacky. It's gross. It shouldn't have happened.'

He arched a brow. 'Because I'm your boss?'

I swallowed so tightly I could hear it. *Gurhdt.* 'Not just that. I'm not…available.' For some reason I couldn't say the word 'married'. I was thoroughly fed up with the word. I wished I never had to hear it again. Married. Yukkety-yuk. Every time I said it I felt sick with shame at how everyone had looked at me back at home when I'd told them the wedding was off. Of course Andy had left that awful task to me. All those exchanged glances that spoke volumes. The I-told-you-something-wasn't-right-about-those-two looks that made my stomach lining corrode with nausea. The pitying looks were the worst. I would do anything to avoid seeing someone look at me that way again.

And I mean *anything*. Including carrying on a charade that was causing me more angst than anything else in my life so far. And that was saying something because my life has not been a tartan-blanket-and-wicker-basket picnic, let me tell you.

Matt's eyes held mine in a lock that made me feel raw and exposed. 'That wasn't the message I've been getting from the moment I met you.'

I was frowning so hard I reckoned even if I'd had Botox in my forehead it would have run off scared.

'I've met men like you before. You get off on the challenge of scoring with someone who's off limits. It's all a game to you. Once you achieve your goal you move on to the next target.' I stepped up close again and poked him in the chest with my index finger. It hurt like hell because his chest was like a wall of marble but I wanted to drive home my point. But on a subconscious level I think I just wanted to touch him again. 'Find someone else to play with, Dr Bishop. I'm off the market. Got it?'

His smile was lazy and his eyes sexily hooded, and trained on my mouth as if he couldn't wait to devour it again. His hand captured mine before I could pull it away and he held it firmly against his chest, right over where his heart was beating. I could feel every thump. The doctor in me couldn't help noticing how fit he was. He had a resting pulse of forty-five bpm, which was pretty damn good. Right now mine was running as if I had arrhythmia. 'If you change your mind, call me,' he said. 'We could make an interesting pair.'

I curled my lip. 'Friends with benefits?'

His eyes glinted. 'Do you need a friend, Dr Clark?'

I needed my head read. That's what I needed. Because when he looked at me like that I wanted to kiss him again. I wanted to push him backwards towards the bed and crawl all over him and climb into his skin. But somehow I managed to get my wild woman back in her cage and snick the lock back in place.

I put up my chin and gave him an icy glare. 'Get your hands off me and keep them off me.'

He held my look for a heart-stopping moment.

I felt the tug of war between our wills. It was like two strong forces that had never encountered that level of oppositional power before. The energy in the air was electric. Supercharged. Crackling like a high-voltage current along a tight wire.

I was the first to look away. I had to otherwise I would have confessed all then and there. But I didn't want his pity. I didn't want him to think I was on the lookout for a rebound fling. That I was so desperate to be found desirable that I would get down and dirty with a man I had known less than twenty-four hours. I wanted to salvage my dignity in the only way I knew how. Pretence. Anyway, I was good at it. I'd been doing it all my life in order to fit in.

I gave my hand an almighty tug and stalked over to where I had left my bag. I shoved it over my shoulder in an affronted manner, tossing my head—even though I know there is no way on earth anyone can *actually* toss their head, or roll their eyes, come to think of it—and wrenched open the suite door.

'Honeymoon over?' he said.

I looked at him over my shoulder. His mouth was lifted in what I was coming to know as his trademark sardonic smile. I let fly with a very rude two-word phrase that basically told him he could…well, I guess you get the idea.

I closed the door with a satisfying snick. I was glad I'd had the last word.

It's not often I get the chance.

CHAPTER FIVE

I'D BEEN HOME half an hour when I suddenly realised how quiet it was. Not just my house, which was like a proverbial tomb—even the rickety floorboards had stopped creaking. No, it was my phone. I would normally get a call from the hospital about a patient, or Jem would text or call or Mum or Dad would check in. Yes, in spite of their anti-capitalist ranting, they both have smartphones.

But nothing. Zilch. *Nada.*

I picked up my bag and searched in its depths for my phone. I usually slip it into one of the inner pockets so I can access it quickly. Sometimes it switches to silent if I'm not careful, or vice versa, which was incredibly embarrassing the last time I went to the cinema. The looks I got! Of course it went off right in the middle of the most important scene in the movie. And it was set on one of my *Looney Tunes* ring tones, which kind of wrecked the poignantly romantic mood.

Anyway, my phone wasn't where I normally put it so I had to go deeper. I swear to God all those jokes about what a woman carries in her handbag are true. I carry my life around in mine. I'm sure one of my shoulders is permanently lower than the other from lugging around the weight of my bag. I fished out my diary—I know there's an electronic one on my phone, but I still like writing things down because I remember them better that way—and then I took out my lip gloss and a wand of mascara and a little pack of tissues with red kisses on them.

I grimaced as I thought of the kisses I'd just exchanged with Matt Bishop. What on earth did he think of me? I had acted like a wanton slut. I had pressed my body against his in the timeless keen-to-mate manner. I'd acted like a tigress in oestrus. It was utterly shameful. What on earth had got into me? I'd been kissed before and nothing like that had happened. In recent times when Andy had kissed me I'd mentally made lists in my head—the wedding invitations, the flowers, the place-setting cards, which aunt to sit next to which aunt—that sort of thing. I had never burst into molten heat like lava blowing out of a volcano.

I tossed the tissues aside and dug deeper. I took out my purse, which is so loaded with loyalty cards I can no longer close it properly. Finally I upended my bag and let everything fall out on the kitchen bench. But apart from a shower of receipts and loose change and the spare key to Jem's place, and two tampons and a furry cough lozenge, there was no phone.

I frowned as I thought of the last time I used it. I didn't have a landline so there was no point in trying to call it. I didn't fancy going out in search of a public phone box, which were as scarce as alley cats with morals in my area. It was too late to knock on Elsie's door to ask to use hers and since Margery Stoneham was away… That's when it hit me. My place wasn't just quiet because my phone was missing.

Where the flipping hell was Freddy?

I called out as I searched in every room. I looked behind doors and in corners. I pulled back the curtains to see if he was playing a game of hide and seek but all I found that was remotely animal-like were dust bunnies. My heart was going into arrhythmia again. I was a cardiac infarct waiting to happen. My hands were shaking and my legs trembling as I stumbled through the rest of the house. Up the stairs I went, calling out at the top of my voice. I didn't care if I woke the neighbours. I didn't care if I woke the dead. I didn't care if I lost my voice in the effort. I had to find that dog! Margery would kill me if anything happened to her precious baby.

I came back down the stairs with a clatter, my feet almost tripping over themselves. I was breathing so hard it sounded like I was wheezing. I was close to crying too but I didn't want to admit it. I'm not a crier. Not any more. Not since the fifth grade in primary school when everyone laughed at my hair. My parents were in their no-shampoo phase. They believed every shampoo and conditioner contained toxic chemicals that would give us all cancer.

We didn't wash our hair with anything but homemade soap for months. Thank God that phase didn't last any longer. Jem and I got head lice, so our parents decided a few toxic chemicals would come in useful after all.

I checked the back garden but there was no sign of Freddy. Even his paw prints in the snow from when I'd

taken him out for a pee before I left with Matt had disappeared as another fresh fall had come down.

I bit my lip to stop it from quivering and rushed back
into the house. He had to be hiding somewhere. A dog
didn't just disappear into midair. This wasn't a science-
fiction show or one of those Las Vegas illusionist's acts.
This was my life! My totally screwball life, admittedly.
I had been watching Freddy the whole time…Or had I?
I had been so worked up about getting outside on the
footpath to wait for Matt. Had I let Freddy out without
realising it? There was no other way he could have got
out. I hadn't left any windows open and, anyway, none
of them were low enough for him to jump out. Could
he have slipped past me without me noticing? He was
only a little dog, and a devious one at that.

I raked my hand through what was now a bird's nest
of my hair. I felt sick and sweaty and icy cold at the
same time. My overactive imagination was conjuring
up horrid images of Freddy squashed flat on Bayswater
Road, or mangled underneath a car and dragged for
miles. Or kidnapped and held for a huge ransom. Or
sold into one of those ghastly fighting dog rings that
operate underground. I choked back a sob as the doorbell rang. It was the police, I was sure of it. They were
here to tell me the dog *I was supposed to be minding*
was deceased.

I wrenched open the door but it wasn't the police.
It was Matt Bishop. For a moment I just looked at him
numbly. The siren of panic screaming in my head had
taken away my ability to speak. I was barely able to
string two thoughts together. My head was pounding

with the effort of trying to keep control of myself and not fall into fits of wild hysteria.

He held up my phone. 'You left it in my car.'

I didn't care about my wretched phone. I took it from him and all but tossed it on the little table in the front hall. 'Have you seen Freddy?' I asked.

His brow furrowed. 'Freddy?'

'The little dog I had in the park,' I said, my breathing still all over the place. 'He's gone. Disappeared. Vanished. I can't find him anywhere.' I could hear my voice cracking and swallowed to clear the blockage of emotion strangling me. 'He must have got out. I have no idea how. He was here when I left with you. I'm sure he was.'

'Where have you looked for him?' Matt asked in a deep, calm voice, which kind of made mine sound all the more hysterical.

'Everywhere,' I said. 'Inside and outside, back and front. He's not *he-e-e-re*.' I dragged 'here' out like a whiny kid having a tantrum. I know. Dead embarrassing.

'What about his owner's house?' he asked. 'Have you looked there?'

I swear to God I could have kissed him. I almost did. I had to physically restrain myself from throwing my arms around his neck and smacking a big fat smoocheroo on his gorgeous mouth. I hadn't thought about Margery's place. It was the most obvious place to look but in my panic I hadn't even thought about it. 'Let's check,' I said instead, and scooped up my coat and scarf off the peg.

I was in such a rush to put it on I got myself in a

tangle. Matt came to the rescue and held my coat behind me like a well-bred gentleman does and helped me guide my arms through the sleeves. Was it my imagination or had his hands given the tops of my shoulders a gentle and reassuring everything-is-going-to-be-all-right squeeze?

For a nanosecond I breathed in the scent of him. I allowed myself a tiny moment of feeling him standing behind me like a strong tower I could lean on. I wasn't used to leaning on anyone for support. I hadn't even let Andy do it, well, because he was rubbish at it, to be honest. But for that tiny fraction of a heartbeat I caught a glimpse of what it would be like to have a partner who would stand by me, who would be strong when I was falling apart, who would take control and sort out the mess I had stumbled into and make it all work out, like unpicking a really hideous knot.

We walked the few houses down to Margery's place. The snow was falling in earnest now. It was really quite romantic, come to think of it. It was like a scene from a film—a guy and a girl walking along the street in search of a missing dog. I just hoped this one had a happy ending.

Matt used the light app on his phone to shine on the footpath so I didn't lose my footing. I guess he must have worked out by now I was pretty clumsy when I got stressed.

When we got to Margery's front porch there was Freddy, sitting on the doormat, shivering so hard he vibrated like a two-stroke engine. I rushed to him without thinking and bundled him into my arms, only to get one of my hands nipped for my trouble. Even though

I was wearing woollen mittens—my ones with kitten faces on them, including whiskers, which might have had something to do with why Freddy attacked me—his teeth sank into my flesh almost to the bone. Well, not quite to the bone, but it sure felt like it.

'Ouch!' I said another word, actually, but you get the idea.

Freddy jumped out of my arms—I might have dropped him but I'm not sure—and started whining and scratching at Margery's front door.

'Are you okay?' Matt asked.

I shoved my hand in my pocket. 'Fine.' I looked at the pathetic sight of the shivering dog desperately trying to get inside his house and felt a wave of compassion flow over me. 'Poor little boy. He misses his mum.'

'Separation anxiety,' Matt said. 'It's because his owner treats him like a human instead of a dog.'

I glanced at him in the light being cast from the streetlight. His face was cast in shadow but the light was still strong enough to show the dark, unreadable sockets of his eyes and the long blade of his nose and his unbelievably gorgeous mouth. 'Yes, well, Freddy is all Margery has now her husband is dead. She has no family other than a sister who doesn't let her bring Freddy with her when she visits so what sort of sister is she?'

'I once minded my sister's pet rat. That's sisterly love for you. I hate the things, but I did it because I love her.' I guess the throbbing pain in my hand was making me run off at the mouth or something. I finally got my motor mouth under control and gave Matt a sheepish look from beneath my half-mast lashes. 'Sorry. Rant over.'

He gave me one of his crooked smiles. 'No problem.'

I looked back at Freddy. 'So, little guy, we'd better come to some sort of understanding. I'm filling in for your mum so you have to do things my way. No more Houdini pranks, okay?'

Matt produced Freddy's lead, which he had wisely taken from my hall table. I'd been in too much of a state to even think about it. He snapped it on the dog's collar and led him away from Margery's front door. 'I'll walk back with you,' he said.

I felt foolish and embarrassed as we walked back to my house. In the last thirty-six hours I had given Matt Bishop an impression of myself that was comical rather than competent. Panicky rather than professional. And—even worse—sexually available instead of committed.

I considered telling him about my cancelled wedding. I had just enough time in the distance between Margery's house and mine. Surely he would understand, given what he'd hinted regarding his parents' marriage? What if I just told him about my stupid postcard fiasco and how I'd been caught off guard when I'd arrived at work? How I had felt too embarrassed to explain and lied to save face. It was a perfectly understandable reaction. I wasn't the first person in the world to utter a little white lie or two. Maybe he'd told a few himself. Surely he'd understand. Who didn't tell a few lies now and again? It was part of being human.

I formed the words in my head but I couldn't get them past my lips. I couldn't bear to tell anyone, least of all him. I felt sick at the thought of it spreading throughout the hospital. I could just imagine the looks I would get. The behind-the-hand comments people would murmur. I had seen the gossip network operate in every hospital I'd worked in. It was the same as the schoolyard network. It was cruel and unstoppable.

I thought of the way Matt had criticised my research project. I couldn't bear to have him mock my personal life as well.

Besides, I wanted to keep my distance from him. He was far too potent for me to handle. He was clearly a man of the world. The world in which his father moved, one where women were prizes to be collected, toys to be played with and then discarded when they lost their appeal. He might have given the impression he didn't approve of his father's treatment of his mother, but wasn't he doing the very same thing with me? He knew I was off limits and yet he'd kissed me. He'd made the first move…hadn't he? Or even if he hadn't he had been the one who had come and stood right in front of me, looking at me in that intensely mesmerising way until I'd had no choice but to meet him halfway.

I wasn't used to feeling such wild, out-of-control feelings of lust and longing. I needed time to get my self-control reconditioned.

We came to my door and I took Freddy's lead from Matt's hand. Even though we were both wearing gloves I felt the jolt of his touch. It travelled through my body like a hot wire firing up my core so it was thrumming like a tuning fork.

'Erm, thanks for helping me find Freddy,' I said. 'I don't know what I would've done if we hadn't found him. He might've frozen to death.'

He looked at me for a long moment. 'It's a big responsibility, minding someone's pet for them. Did you offer or did your neighbour pressure you?'

How had he guessed that? I wondered. I shifted my weight from foot to foot, suddenly uncomfortable he was sensing more about me than I cared to have on show. 'I was just trying to help.'

He gave a nod as if that made sense. 'I'd better get going before I freeze to death. Good night.'

I watched him walk down my street from my front door. It was bitterly cold standing there on the doorstep but I couldn't take my eyes off his tall, rangy figure as he walked along the snow-covered footpath. I let out a long, foggy breath as he disappeared around the corner.

Oh, boy, was I in trouble.

I was in the female change room, putting my bag in the locker, the next morning when Gracie McCurcher came bursting in. 'Guess what?' she said, her eyes bright with conspiratorial excitement.

'What?'

'Matt Bishop has a girlfriend.'

I hoped my face hadn't shown my surprise. If he had a girlfriend then why the heck had he kissed me last night? I felt a rumble of anger roll through me. What was it about me that attracted two-timing guys? Did I have a sign on my head that said 'Exploit me'?

I shoved my bag in the locker and turned the key. 'How do you know?'

'He's got a hickey on his neck,' Gracie said. 'I saw it when he took off his scarf when he came in this morning.'

I was glad I was facing the locker bay instead of

Gracie. I was so hot in the face I was sure the lockers would melt and drool, like Salvador Dali's clock. 'Are you sure it's a hickey?' I said in a vaguely interested way. 'He might have scratched himself shaving.'

'I know a hickey when I see one,' Gracie said. 'I wonder who it is? Do you reckon it's someone from the hospital?'

'I have no idea.' I was scaring myself at how easy it was to lie.

Gracie was watching me in the mirror, where I was attempting to put my hair in some sort of order. 'I heard he went to the US after he broke up with a long-term girlfriend. She was a speech pathologist.'

'How long term?' I asked.

'Not sure.' Gracie gave me a speaking glance. 'For some men a couple of weeks is long term.'

I turned around and gave her arm a squeeze. She hadn't had much luck with boyfriends. Her first one left her for her best friend and her last one cheated on her the whole time they were together. She was a lot like me, she wanted the fairytale but so far it had eluded her. 'Don't give up hope, Gracie,' I said. 'You'll find your handsome prince one day.'

She gave me a thoughtful look. 'Is it better once you're married?'

I disguised a gulping swallow. 'Better?'

'Your relationship,' she said. 'More stable. Secure. Happier. My cousin told me she felt really let down after she got married. She said there's all that build-up to the big day. Months and months of planning and then it's all over. Was it like that for you?'

'A little, I guess,' I said, which at least was the truth. I was let down. Massively. Everything I had planned and dreamed for myself had been blown away as soon as I'd opened that bedroom door and seen Andy in bed with another woman. Someone younger and far more beautiful than I could ever be. And taller and thinner. She looked like one of those bikini models on a billboard. I'd felt short and dowdy and fat ever since.

'When can I see the photos?' Gracie asked. 'Have you got time now?'

'Sorry.' I glanced at the clock on the wall. 'I have to get going. I have to check on a patient before Theatre.'

I came back from Theatre and Jill Carter, the ward clerk, looked up from some filing she was doing. 'Have you heard the latest gossip?' She shut the filing-cabinet drawer and gave the same conspiratorial gleam Gracie had shown earlier.

I prided myself on my indifferent expression. I'd been practising behind my surgical mask in Theatre. 'No.'

'Apparently Dr Bishop is—'

'Right behind you,' Matt said from the office doorway.

Jill and I both turned around like schoolgirls caught out smoking behind the toilets. Jill recovered quicker than I did but, then, she probably hadn't spent half the night lying awake fantasising about his mouth kissing her.

'Oh, hello, Dr Bishop,' she said, smiling brightly. 'How did your heads of department meeting go?'

Matt's expression had the high wall with barbed wire

at the top look about it. 'Fine. Dr Clark?' His gaze nailed mine. 'My office in ten minutes.'

I couldn't stop my gaze drifting to his neck. His shirt collar covered half of it but anyone with a history of necking as a teenager would have recognised it for what it was. I could feel the slow, hot crawl of colour spread over my cheeks as my eyes came back to his. 'Sure,' I said. 'I'll just check on a couple of patients first.'

I was longer than ten minutes as I wanted to talk to Jason Ryder's parents about a new type of therapy I was keen to use with him. Childhood awakening therapy was still in its experimental stage but there was some anecdotal evidence of people in comas responding to stimuli from their childhoods. Playing music, favourite movies or reading well-loved childhood stories had produced responses in some patients. I felt sure it wouldn't compromise the care Jason was already receiving, and I was quietly confident it might be the key to getting him to wake. From what I'd gathered from his parents, he'd had a happy and contented childhood, which made him a perfect candidate.

Jason's parents were keen to try anything to get their boy to wake up and his young wife, Megan, was also supportive. I didn't want to offer them false hope but I was keen to try whatever I could to get the break-through everyone was hoping and praying for. The human brain had much more plasticity than the scientific community had realised up until recent times. It was an exciting time to be involved with neurosurgery as there were new techniques and advances in technology that brought relief and hope to patients who in the past would have had little or no hope of recovery.

I was on my way to Matt's office twenty-five minutes later when Professor Cleary stopped me in the corridor. He was Head of Geriatrics and I generally avoided him as I found him so negative. He drained my energy if I hung around him too long. I often wondered how his patients put up with his bedside manner. I always had to remind myself to call him Professor Cleary instead of Dreary. One of the residents almost got fired when he let slip the nickname on a ward round.

But this time Prof Cleary wasn't frowning or glowering in his usual doom-and-gloom manner. 'Hello, Bertie,' he said with a broad smile. 'I've been hearing about your research project at the heads of department meeting.' He gave a chuckle. 'Best joke I've heard in years.'

I lifted my chin and eyeballed him. 'What did you find so amusing about it?'

'S.C.A.M.' He chuckled again, a deep belly laugh that made the already frayed edges of my nerves rub raw. 'Harrison Redding is kicking himself for not seeing it earlier. Clever of you to poke fun at the establishment like that. But it won't win you any favours with the boss. He's a sharp tack, isn't he? Got a good reputation for getting the job done. You'll have to watch yourself. I can't see him letting you read his palm or his aura or whatever else it is you do.'

I clenched my jaw so hard it clicked audibly. I didn't respond other than to give him a hard, tight smile and continued on my way to Matt's office. But the sound of Professor Cleary's chuckle followed me all the way down the corridor.

My skin rose in a hot prickle. Who else would be laughing at me by the end of the day? I had walked

down a lot of corridors during my childhood and ado-
lescence with that sound ringing in my ears. My face
boiled with embarrassment. I was furious with Matt but
I was even more furious with myself. I had set myself
up for mockery and I hadn't even realised it.

Honestly, a transactional analysis psychologist could
conduct a whole conference on me.

I knocked on Matt's door and he issued a curt command to come in. I stepped inside his office to see him
sitting behind his desk with a grim look on his face.
'You're late.'

I pulled my shoulders back. Jem calls it my bracing-
for-a-punch-up pose. I wouldn't know the first thing
about throwing a punch but I can look intimidating
when I have to. Well, sort of. 'I'm not at your beck and
call, Dr Bishop,' I said. 'I have responsibilities and commitments that have nothing whatsoever to do with you.
And while I'm on the subject of commitments and responsibilities, you had no right to use my project title
as a source of amusement at your heads of department
meeting.'

A challenging light came into his grey-blue eyes.
'Are you asking to be fired?'

I held his look with equal force. 'Are you threatening me?'

His eyes moved over my face, settling on my mouth
as if he was remembering how it felt against his own.
I couldn't stop myself from moistening my lips. It was
an instinctive reaction and my belly quivered when I
saw him follow the movement.

His eyes came back to mine and I heard him release
a short, whooshy sort of breath, as if he'd had a long,

trying day. 'I wasn't responsible for that,' he said. 'One of the other department heads commented on it. It created a few laughs, sure, but I encouraged everyone to stick to the agenda. What you need to concentrate on is producing data.'

I wasn't ready to be mollified even if he had stood up for me, which I very much doubted. I could imagine him smirking along with the rest of them, having a laugh at my expense. 'I don't appreciate being the butt of puerile boardroom jokes,' I said. 'My research is important to me and I know it can bring about better outcomes. I just need time to prove it.'

'I have no issue with that,' he said. 'But that's not why I asked you to come in here.'

I hooked one of my eyebrows upwards. Jem calls it my schoolmarm look. *'Asked?'* I said. 'Don't you mean commanded?'

He gave me a levelling look. 'One of the nurses mentioned you're planning to do some extra therapy with Jason Ryder. I'd like you to explain to me exactly what it is you intend to do.'

I could see the scepticism in his expression. He had already made up his mind. He would rubbish my childhood awakening therapy like he'd rubbished my project. 'What would be the point?' I said. 'You'll just call it a whole lot of hocus-pocus.'

'Hocus-pocus it may well be, but I would still like to know about it first rather than hear it second-hand from a junior nurse. That is not how I want to run this department.'

The clipped censure in his tone made my back come up. I could feel every knob of my spine tightening like a wrench on a bolt. 'Even scientists have to have open minds, Dr Bishop. Otherwise they can be blinded by bias. They only see what they expect to see.'

His eyes battled with mine as his hands came down hard on the desk in front of him. 'I'll tell you what I expect to see, Dr Clark. Patients being treated with proven, testable treatments, not sprinkled with fairy dust or having crystals waved over them. I'm running an ICU department here, not a freaking New Age mind and body expo.'

I clenched my fists by my sides to stop myself from grabbing him by the front of his shirt. 'Is there any space in that closed mind of yours for good old-fashioned hope? Or do you always expect the worst just to keep your back covered?'

A muscle moved in and out in his jaw as he straightened from the desk. 'It's not fair to offer hope when there is none. People's lives—the ones left behind—get ruined by empty promises. Jason's family needs reliable information and support right now, not sorcery.'

My eyes flared in outrage. I was so incensed I wanted to hit something. 'Is that all you wanted to see me about? Because, if not, I have some spells to work on in my cauldron.'

A flicker of amusement momentarily disrupted the hardened line of his mouth. I got the feeling he was trying not to laugh. Somehow that made my anger cool a little. I liked it that he had a sense of humour. I liked it a lot more than I wanted to admit. 'There's one other thing,' he said.

I folded my arms like a sulky teenager. I even pushed my bottom lip out in a pout. I know it was childish but he deserved it. *Sorcery?* Good grief. I hadn't been to one of my parents' seances in months. 'What?'

'We have a situation.'

'We do?'

I was the one with A Situation. It was getting more and more ridiculous by the minute. Why, oh, why had I been so wretchedly cowardly about being jilted? Why hadn't I told everyone the truth right from the start? I felt like all my lies had followed me into his office. They were stealing all the oxygen out of the air. It was like being in an overcrowded lift. I was finding it hard to breathe when he looked at me in that all-seeing way.

'Last night—'

'Was a mistake and it won't be repeated,' I said, before he could go any further. 'I can't believe I did that... we did that. I blame it on the champagne. I never drink on an empty stomach. It was totally out of character and I apologise for any...' my eyes glanced briefly at his neck '...erm...inconvenience.'

His eyes continued to hold mine but his gave nothing away. It was like a drawbridge had come up. 'I like to keep my private life out of the corridors of the hospital.'

'Because of your ex?' I said.

A flash of something hard moved in his gaze. 'As I said, I like to keep my private life private.'

'Fine. Me too.'

He gave me a long, measuring look. 'If people were to put two and two together, things could get rather awkward for you.'

They couldn't get any more awkward than they already are, I thought. 'How is anyone going to know that what happened last night had anything to do with me?'

His poker face was back on but I was pretty sure there was a glint of amusement lurking in the back of his gaze. 'So I take it you didn't tell your husband?'

I pressed my lips together. 'No.'

'Why not?'

'Because…he wouldn't understand.' It sounded like a tawdry cliché. The bored and lonely, misunderstood wife looking for a bit of fun on the side.

Matt came around his desk and perched on one corner, his ankles crossed, his arms folded across the broad expanse of his chest. It was the sort of casual but in-command pose that signified a man who knew what he wanted and exactly how to get it.

It hit me then.

He wanted me.

I saw it in the gleam of his eyes as they held mine. I felt it in the electric charge of the air we shared. I felt it in the core of my body where a throb had started like a low, deep ache, slowly building to a pulsating need that radiated throughout my system. I folded my arms, as if that would help contain the fire that was raging in my blood.

'Have you thought about my offer?' he asked.

I swallowed tightly. 'Um…your offer of what?'

His eyes tethered mine. 'Exploring this thing between us.'

This thing between us… It was more than a thing. It was taking me over. My insides coiled with desire. I wanted him as much as he wanted me. The thought of an illicit affair with him was suddenly very tempting. I'd had such a boring sex life. This would be my chance to stretch my boundaries a bit. Gain a bit more experience with a man who truly wanted me. I could throw off my inhibitions and have a fling, like every other girl my age.

But how could I agree to such a thing while he thought I was married?

I unfolded my arms and held them stiffly by my sides, shooting him a caustic glare. 'I suppose you think just because I allowed you to kiss me that it means I'm desperate to jump into bed with you. Well, guess what? I'm not. Going to jump into bed with you or kiss you or allow you to touch me or even look at me like that.'

'Look at you like what?'

I glowered at him through eyes so narrowed I could barely see out of them. It was like peering through the eye of an embroidery needle. 'You know exactly what I mean. You're doing it now. You're looking at me as if you'd like to strip me naked and have me on your desk.'

I really should think before I speak. It's a bad habit of mine. The erotic premise of my words filled the air with a crackling tension that made the hairs on the back of my neck lift. The heat of his gaze seared its way through my body to gather in a molten pool between my legs. I even felt the skin on my body tingle and tickle all over, like the rapid spread of goose bumps.

In fact, I don't think I'd ever been more aware of my body before that moment. All my erogenous zones— including some I hadn't known I had—were flashing red hot, like a computer motherboard malfunctioning. My breasts tightened behind the lace shield of my bra. They felt twice their size—which would have been fabulous if it were physically possible—and overly sensitive. My mouth ached to feel his against it, in it, conquering it, devouring it. I ran the tip of my tongue over my lips and watched as he tracked its moist passage. My body silently screamed for him to close the distance, to crush his mouth to mine and do exactly as I'd so crudely said.

He moved away from the desk and came a step closer. I should have stepped back but, just like the time before, my feet felt clamped to the floor. He lifted my chin with the tip of his finger, just like those romantic heroes do in the movies. No one had ever done that to me before, which was kind of why I was acting so bunny-in-the-headlights. His fingertip felt warm and strong and yet gentle at the same time. I felt the tingle of his touch all the way to my toes. His gaze locked on mine, his pupils flared to deep pools of black ink. 'What are you doing for dinner this evening?' he asked.

I glared at him even harder, which was quite hard to do with him that close and smelling so lemony and citrusy. 'Did you even *hear* what I just said?'

'I'm free if you are.'

I tried for my best haughty tone. 'It's none of your business what I'm doing.'

'You made it my business by kissing me.'

'I did *not* kiss you!' I stamped my foot for emphasis. 'You kissed me. I just responded, which is perfectly understandable given I'd had a full glass of champagne.'

His eyes smouldered darkly as they held mine. 'How about we try it without the champagne this time? See if we get the same response. That would be more scientific, wouldn't you agree?'

I should have got away while I could but before I knew it his hands were on my upper arms and his mouth was on mine. It was a hard kiss, a proving-the-point kiss, but it was no less mind-blowing. My mouth opened under the heated pressure of his, my tongue mating with his in an erotic duel that made my insides shiver with lust.

I was hardly aware of doing so but suddenly my arms were snaking around his neck, my fingers lacing through the silky thickness of his hair as his mouth plundered mine. My breasts were so tightly jammed against him I could feel my nipples poking into his chest. My pelvis was on fire; I moved it against his in an attempt to assuage the grinding, empty ache of my body. His erection surged against me, potent and hard, powerful and dangerously tempting. I imagined him entering me, dividing my moist, hungry flesh and driving hard and repeatedly into me. I was so turned on I could feel the tingle of arousal tightening my core, the sensitive nerves pulsing in anticipation.

His hands cradled my head, his fingers strong and firm against my scalp. His teeth nipped and pulled at my lower lip, cajoling me into a payback game that made the base of my spine splinter into a million pieces like party glitter. I could barely stand upright. The sensations were earth-shattering as they coursed through me like the shot of a powerful drug. I was so pliable in his arms I was like a rag doll. I was melting into his hard frame as if I never wanted to be separate from him. I wanted to be fused to his body, to have him possess me and make me feel alive in a way I had never quite managed before.

'God, this is crazy,' he said against my mouth. I loved the tickling and tingling sensation his words created against my lips. It had an incendiary effect on me, making me kiss him with all the more shameful, wanton enthusiasm. I went back in search of his tongue, warring with it, teasing it to come and play with me.

His hands slid down my body to grasp me by the hips, his fingers digging into my flesh as if he never wanted to let me go. I could feel the throb of his arousal against me. It excited me to think I'd had that effect on him. But his hands didn't stay for long on my hips. One went to the base of my spine to bring me hard against him while the other cupped my breast through my clothes. It wasn't enough for me. I wanted his mouth on my breast. I tugged my shirt out of my jeans and guided his hand to my lace-covered breast.

He stroked his thumb over my budded nipple, creating a maelstrom of sensation that travelled through my body. He pushed my padded bra out of the way and lowered his head and took my breast in his mouth. Yes, it's actually small enough to do that. Well, maybe not quite all the way into his mouth, but you get the idea. But it didn't seem to matter to him that my breast was a little on the small side. He treated it like it was the most gorgeously ripe breast in the world. Seriously, you would've thought it was a Playboy Bunny's breast. His tongue played with my nipple, circling it and teasing it into a tight pucker. I tilted back my head as he moved his mouth over the upper curve of my breast.

He did the same to the under-curve, which was even more tantalising. I hadn't realised how sensitive my skin was there until his warm mouth and the sexily raspy skin of his chin and jaw moved against it.

He left my breast to come back to my mouth, subjecting it to a passionate onslaught that had me breathless and throbbing from head to toe with longing. I was aching with the need to have him inside me. I hadn't even felt this turned on as a teenager. It was like discovering my female hormones for the first time. They were surging through my system like an unstoppable force. I wanted him and I wanted him now.

One of my hands went for the waistband of his trousers but he stilled my hand, pressing it against the turgid length of him. 'Not here,' he said.

The words brought me back to my senses like a slap across the cheek. What was I doing, undressing my boss in his office? What was *wrong* with me? Besides the fact he thought I was married, I wasn't the type of girl to act so unprofessionally. I was annoyed that he was the one to bring things to a halt. In my mind it gave him the moral edge, making him far more principled than me. It made me feel as if I was the one who had no self-control, which was a whole lot nearer to the truth than I wanted it to be.

I relied on my usual cover-up tactic and gave him a disparaging look. 'Do you really think I was going to let this go further than a kiss and a quick grope?'

His eyes were a dark blue-grey as they held mine, the pupils still widened in arousal. 'If you change your mind you know where to find me. I'll be home all evening.'

I drew in a scalding breath. 'You'll be waiting a long time before I make a house call.'

A hint of a smile lifted the edges of his mouth. 'We'll see.' He went back around his desk and rolled out his chair. His eyes glinted as he added, 'Close the door on your way out, will you?'

I huffed and puffed for a moment before I whipped round and stomped out of his office, but I didn't close the door.

I slammed it.

CHAPTER SIX

'GOOD GRACIOUS, BERTIE.' Stuart McTaggart jumped about a foot in the air as the framed prints rattled on the wall as he came towards me. 'What on earth's the matter?'

I pressed my lips together so tightly they hurt. 'Nothing,' I muttered.

'Is it about your project?' He gave a chuckle not unlike Professor Cleary's. It was the first time I'd heard him laugh, so at least I'd achieved something, I thought wryly. 'I thought it was brilliant, actually. Very witty.'

'I can assure you it wasn't meant to be,' I said, as I walked down the corridor with him.

'I've just been in to see Jason Ryder,' Stuart said. 'His parents mentioned you want to try some new therapy with him.'

'That's if Dr Bishop will allow it,' I said through tight lips.

Stuart stopped walking to look at me. 'But he was very supportive of you in the meeting. He was the one who brought the meeting to order when we were all having a laugh about your research title. In fact, if I didn't know you'd just come back from your honeymoon I would've said you and he were an item. Did you see that love bite on his neck?' He gave another chuckle. 'Takes me back to my old courting days.'

I could feel my blush like a spreading fire. 'Personally, I think love bites are dreadfully tacky.'

He gave a grunt and continued walking. 'So, what have you got in mind for Jason?'

I explained what I planned to do and he listened— patiently, for him—before giving me the go-ahead. 'Can't see how it can hurt,' he said. He waited a beat before adding, 'I hope to God the family don't sue.'

I glanced at his worried expression. 'They don't seem the type and, besides, you didn't do anything wrong. It's a recognised complication of that type of neurosurgery.'

'Doesn't seem to matter to litigation lawyers, does it?' He gave me a cynical look. 'They want their pound of flesh and don't care who they slice it off.'

'I'm sure it won't come to that, Stuart,' I said, hoping it was true. Stuart was a highly competent surgeon but his gruff and autocratic manner often put people off side. When things went wrong, which they occasionally did because that kind of surgery on the human body wasn't an exact science, some people thought their only option was to sue for damages, but they didn't take into account the impact on the doctor.

Medicine today was far more of a team approach than in the past. Mistakes could be made anywhere along the chain of care but it was the doctor who ended up being the fall guy. It was especially difficult if the case was reported in the press. Biased reporting could smear a doctor's reputation, tearing down a lifetime of hard work in a sensationalised phrase or two. And then there was the well-documented expert witness dripping with hindsight bias. And coroners' cases, in which months could be taken over dissecting decisions that doctors had to make under pressure, in real time, with incomplete information in a badly constructed system. Insurance companies battled it out with their case-hardened lawyers but the doctor, usually with no medico-legal experience, was left as the scapegoat, with often devastating psychological fallout.

At my previous hospital a dedicated obstetrician had walked away from a thirty-year career after parents of a baby who suffered oxygen deprivation at birth and subsequent brain damage sued her for damages. The sensationalised reporting in the press besmirched her reputation to such a degree she felt she could no longer practise.

Stuart let out a tired-sounding sigh. 'Well, I'd better get a move on. I've got a clinic and then a tutorial with the students and I'm on call for the second time this week. It's a wonder my wife doesn't call a divorce lawyer.' He gave me a sideways glance. 'How does your husband cope with the demands of your job?'

'Erm...'

'Should've married a doctor, Bertie.'

I gave him one of my strained smiles. 'There's a thought.'

For the next week I changed my roster to night shifts. I know it was cowardly but I really wasn't ready to face Matt Bishop until I got my willpower under some semblance of control. Besides, there's nothing more lust deadening than lack of sleep. One good side of working the night shift was that I could walk Freddy in daylight… I use the word loosely because the sort of daylight we get in London in January is pretty insipid.

The other benefit of being on night duty was that I could spend a bit more time with patients without the hustle and bustle of ward rounds and relatives visiting. ICU was quiet all but for the hiss and groan of ventilators or beeping of heart monitors and heart-lung machines.

I sat by Jason Ryder's bed in the end room and watched as his chest rose and fell with the action of the ventilator. It was coming up to two weeks since his surgery and he was still in a deep coma, and every time we had tried to bring him out of it his brain pressures had skyrocketed. It wasn't looking good but I refused to give up hope. I couldn't get his wife, Megan, out of my mind. I could imagine how devastating it was for her to be expecting a baby at a time like this. The stress she was under wasn't good for her or the baby. Studies indicated that high cortisol levels in expectant mothers could cause epigenetic changes in the foetus, leaving them at higher risk of heart disease or some types of cancers in later life.

And then there were Jason's parents. I could imagine how my parents would feel if either Jem or I were in a coma. They would be frantic with worry, desperate for some thread of hope. No parent wanted to outlive his or her child. It wasn't the natural order of things. Every time I looked at Jason's parents I felt a pressing ache inside my chest, like a stack of bricks pressing down on my heart. I so wanted a good outcome for them and for Jason, who'd had such a bright future ahead of him.

I picked up the children's book Jason's parents had left earlier. It was one of my own favourites, *The Indian in the Cupboard* by Lynne Reid Banks. Apparently Jason had loved it when he'd been about nine or ten years old. I, too, remembered being captivated by the idea of a toy coming to life. I picked up where Jason's mother had left off before they'd left for the night and read a few pages.

I looked up after a few minutes to see Matt Bishop standing in the doorway, watching me. I had no idea how long he'd been there. I hadn't seen his name on the night-shift roster but, then, he might have been called in for a patient. I knew he worked ridiculously long hours. It had taken me quite an effort to avoid running into him. I even darted into the broom cupboard next to the doctors' room a couple of evenings ago when I heard him speaking with a colleague around the corner.

I can tell you I got a bit worried when he stopped right outside it and talked to Brian Kenton from Radiology. I had a sneaking suspicion he might have known I was in there. He took an inordinately long time to discuss a patient before moving on. I felt a fool, sneaking out of there a few minutes later, but what else could I have done?

I put the book down on the bedside table and rose to my feet. 'Did you want me—I mean something?' I asked, mentally cursing the fact I was blushing.

'How's he doing?'

'Much the same,' I said. 'His IC pressures spike every time I try to wean him off the ventilator. Stuart wants to keep them low to maximise perfusion of what might be marginally viable brain around the tumour bed. But before we ramp up sedation each time, there's no sign of consciousness. He's having another CT tomorrow to look at perfusion. And an EEG is planned after that.'

I handed him the notes, which he read through with a frown of concentration pulling at his brow. He drew in a deep breath, closed the notes and put them back on the end of the bed. He picked up the children's book and turned over a few pages. 'I remember reading this when I was about eight or nine.'

'I read it too,' I said. 'I can tell you I never looked at a toy the same way again.'

His mouth curved upwards in a half-smile as he tapped the book against his hand. 'So, this is part of your childhood awakening therapy?'

I searched his features for any sign of mockery but he was either keeping it under wraps or was genuinely giving me a fair and unbiased hearing. Or maybe he'd looked up some of the fledgling research online and was prepared to keep an open mind. 'Reading familiar stories, playing favourite music, relating family memories of holidays or whatever to the patient can sometimes trigger an emotional response,' I said. 'There've been a few cases reported now where patients have woken from comas when exposed to something particularly emotive from their childhood.'

'One assumes it would be beneficial to have a happy childhood in order to expect that sort of response.'

I frowned. 'You didn't have a happy childhood?' I asked it as a question, but it could easily have been a statement of observation, given the way his features were set.

'Not particularly.' He put the book back on the bedside table before he gave me a little quirk of a smile. 'What about you?'

'Mostly.' I gave him a rueful look and then added, 'My parents are a little out there, if you know what I mean.'

'I would never have guessed.'

I couldn't help a short laugh escaping. 'I'm ultra-conservative compared to them. At least I turn up at work fully clothed.'

His eyes darkened as they meshed with mine. 'What time's your break?'

I glanced at my watch. 'Ten minutes ago.'

He took my elbow with a firm but surprisingly gentle hand. 'Come on. Boss's orders. Caffeine and sugar.'

We took our coffee and a packet of chocolate biscuits to his office. I got the feeling this was his way of calling a truce. He pulled out his office chair for me to sit on. 'Here, you play the boss for a while. Tell me how you would do things around here if you were me.'

I sat on his chair but I'm so short my feet didn't reach the floor. I tucked my ankles beneath its centre stand and hoped he wouldn't notice. I took a sip of coffee and looked at him over the rim of my cup. He was sitting in the chair I'd used the last time, his features showing the signs of the stresses of his job.

It looked like he hadn't shaved in over eighteen hours, his eyes had damson-coloured shadows beneath them, his hair was ruffled, as if he'd recently combed it with his fingers, and there were two lines down each side of his mouth I hadn't noticed before. I knew for a fact he wasn't on that evening because I'd checked.

After the broom cupboard hideout I wasn't taking any chances. He had worked day shifts for the last week, presumably so he could keep in closer touch with the hospital management staff while he ironed out the problems he'd inherited.

It made me wonder if he had anything outside work to distract him. A hobby or interest that gave him some respite from the human tragedy he dealt with day in, day out.

He was a dedicated workaholic. The type A personality who found it hard to be anything but task-oriented. Emotions were not to be trusted. It was facts and data and completing the job that motivated him. I knew from my study how important it was to search for balance. I'm not sure I had found it, given the way things had turned out between Andy and me, but at least I understood the dynamic.

I was starting to realise why Matt had taken such a stand with me on that first day. For a man who valued facts over feelings I must have come across as a complete nut job. He wanted the unit to be one of the best in the country, if not the world.

No wonder he had taken the line he had with me. I was like a loaded cannon to him. Someone who was unpredictable, perhaps even—in his opinion—unstable. I had some ground to make up to make him see me as the dedicated professional I was. Sure, I wore wacky clothes and did interesting things with my hair, but that didn't mean I wasn't a competent and committed anaesthetist. I took my responsibility with patients seriously. I literally had their lives in my hands. I would never do anything to compromise their safety. I just had to convince Matt Bishop I wasn't the airy-fairy flake he thought I was.

I put my coffee cup down. God knows I sure didn't need the caffeine. My heart was already pounding as if I'd had a dozen espressos with an energy drink chaser. Matt had that sort of effect on me. 'I'm sorry about the other day in your office,' I said.

'No apology necessary.' He sat watching me with his steady, measuring gaze, his coffee cup cradled in his right hand, one ankle crossed over his knee.

I glanced longingly at the chocolate biscuits on the desk but I knew if I started on them I might not stop till the whole packet was gone. My parents banning sugar had had the unfortunate effect of making me a sugar binger. I could eat a box of chocolates in one sitting, especially if I was feeling down about myself. I just hoped my liver wasn't going to hate me for it some time in the future.

Matt leaned forward and pushed the packet of biscuits closer. 'Go on. One won't hurt.'

I gave him a twisted smile as I took a biscuit out of the packet. 'My mum does that.'

'What?'

'Reads minds.'

He smiled back. It relaxed his tired and drawn features and made me realise all over again how incredibly attractive he was. I looked at the biscuit in my hand rather than look at his mouth, as I was so tempted to do. All I could think of was how his mouth felt as it moved against mine, how his hands had felt, touching my body. How I wanted him to touch me again. How I wanted to feel his body inside mine, making me come apart with ecstasy.

I was shocked at my behaviour. Shocked and bewildered. If my life had gone according to plan I would now be married and trying for a baby. Instead, I was single and feverishly attracted to a man I had only met a matter of two weeks ago. It was like my body had hijacked my mind. It was acting on its own initiative, responding and sending subtle and some not-so-subtle signals to him that I was attracted to him and available. No wonder he had offered me an affair. I would have to try harder to disguise my reaction to him. Definitely no more getting close to him. And absolutely *no* touching. I would have to limit my time alone with him, keeping things on a professional basis at all times.

I took a small nibble of my biscuit and chewed and swallowed it, acutely conscious of his steady gaze resting on me.

'You mentioned your parents are alternative,' he said. 'How alternative?'

'They're hippies,' I said. 'They both come from families with money, but for as long as I can remember they've moved from place to place around the country, following whatever lifestyle guru takes their fancy, or their money, or both.'

'Not an easy way to spend your childhood.'

I rolled my eyes. 'Tell me about it. There's only so much teasing or tofu a kid can take. But don't get me wrong. My parents are really cool people. I love them dearly and I totally understand their desire to live an alternative lifestyle. They're not the sort of people who could ever do the nine-to-five suburban thing. It's just not the way I want to live my life.'

'How did you cope, growing up?'

I gave him one of my sheepish looks. 'I rebelled now and again.'

'How?'

'I became a closet carnivore.'

He laughed. 'Wicked girl.'

I smiled back. He had such a nice laugh. Deep and rich and full-bodied, like a top-shelf wine. Seriously, I could get drunk on hearing it. 'I can still taste my first steak,' I said. 'What an awesome moment that was. Jem and I used to sneak out at night, not to sleep with boys or drink alcohol, like normal girls did. We'd find a restaurant and indulge ourselves in a feast of medium-rare steak.'

He put his coffee cup on the desk, a smile still curving his lips. 'Did your parents ever find out?'

'Not so far.' I licked the chocolate off my fingers. 'I'm good at keeping secrets.'

'Handy talent to have.' There was a glint in his eye that made something in my stomach quiver like an unset jelly.

I looked away and buried my nose in my coffee cup. I couldn't envisage how I was ever going to confess my folly. The only way I could think to wriggle out of it would be to put in my resignation and start over in a new hospital. It was the only way to save face. But the thought of resigning and reapplying somewhere else was daunting. I loved working at St Iggy's. It was the first place I'd felt as if I belonged. I was part of a team that brought top-quality health care to the public, and the fact that I had—so far—been allowed to trial some alternative therapies was an added bonus.

I put my coffee cup down with a little clatter. 'I'd better get back to work. Thanks for the coffee.'

'You're welcome.'

I walked to the door but before I could put my hand on the doorknob to open it his hand got there first. My hand brushed against his and I pulled it back as if I'd been zapped. His right arm was stretched out against the back of my right shoulder. I could smell the grace notes of his aftershave as well as his own warm male smell, which was even more intoxicating.

I made the mistake of looking up at him. Our eyes met in a timeless moment that swirled and throbbed with sensual undertones I could feel reverberating in my body.

His gaze dropped to my mouth. 'You have chocolate on your lip.'

'I do?' I swept my tongue over my lips. 'Gone?'

He brought the pad of his thumb to my lower lip and gently blotted it. 'Got it.'

Our eyes met again. Held. Burned. Tempted.

I drew in a shaky breath and pulled out of his magnetic field.

I turned and walked down the corridor, but it wasn't until I turned the corner that I heard his door click shut.

CHAPTER SEVEN

AFTER ANOTHER WEEK I was completely over doing night shifts. My circadian rhythms were so out of whack I was practically brain dead. My eyes were so darkly shadowed I looked like I'd walked off the set of a zombie movie. I had a couple of days off, which I spent painting my sitting room, something I'd had to put on hold while I'd had Freddy staying. Margery was back from her sister's now so I could stop worrying about muddy paws and mad yapping, not to mention obsessive chewing.

I'd given Freddy a big marrowbone to chew instead of my shoes and electronic appliance cords, but he'd buried it in the back garden and then brought it in covered in mud and slush and left it on my pillow. Nice.

The time off had also given me some space to work on the hospital ball. I'd gone back to the hotel and talked to the catering manager and I'd ordered the decorations and got posters printed and had them hung around the hospital. The ticket sales had been slow until I had taken over, which was rather gratifying. It seemed everyone was delighted with the idea of a fancy-dress ball and were madly ordering costumes online or in stores.

When I got back to work after my days off I was pleased to hear Jason Ryder had been gradually weaned off the sedation, but while his brain pressures hadn't soared and he was breathing on his own, he was still not responding to verbal commands. I encouraged his family to continue with the therapies I'd suggested and hoped they would see some improvement over the next week or so.

The EEG had encouragingly shown brain activity. There was something going on in Jason's head, but it wasn't getting out, a possible case of 'locked-in syndrome'. But *what* was locked in was still an unknown. Just how much loss of brain function had resulted from the surgery was anyone's guess at this stage.

Matt Bishop was alone in the central ICU office when I came in from checking on Jason. All the nurses, including Gracie, were occupied with patients. Jill was on an errand to another ward and the registrars were with one of the other consultants with a patient in Bay Five.

'Good news so far on Jason,' I said, by way of greeting. I was going to stick to my plan of keeping things professional and distant.

Matt was less optimistic. 'He's not responding to any stimuli.'

'Not yet,' I said. 'But his CT shows reasonable blood flow in most of the brain, and his EEG shows activity.'

He put the file he was holding down on the counter desk and momentarily leaned forward and rested his hands on top of it. There was a deep frown line between his eyes, his olive-toned skin looked even paler than usual and he had a pinched looked about his features.

If a zombie movie director had been looking for walk-on extras, I thought Matt and I would make a great pair.

'Are you okay?' I asked.

He drew in a breath and straightened, rubbing a hand over the back of his neck. 'Fine.'

'You don't look fine.'

'Thanks.'

I peered at him up close. 'Your eyes are bloodshot. Have you been on the turps?'

He gave me a look. 'No. I was up all night. And, no, I wasn't on night shift.'

'At least on night shift you get paid to feel like crap.'

He managed a quarter-smile and then it faded as he dragged his hand down his face this time, wincing as if the movement caused him pain. 'You have no idea of the mess this place is in. Jeff Hooper might win a popularity contest over me any day but he had no idea how to balance a budget. We're four months from the end of the financial year and the budget is blown. The CEO says there is no more money. How the hell can we pay staff and provide a service with an empty bank account? I've been told to come up with a solution.'

I stepped back and folded my arms across my chest before I was tempted to smooth that canyon-deep furrow off his brow. 'Is there anything I can do?'

He looked at me then. *Really* looked at me. His eyes went to mine, holding them in a lock that contained the sensual heat of everything we had experienced together in private—the kisses, the touches, the mutual arousal of primal desire. It went back and forth between our gazes like a fizzing current of electricity. I swear it was almost audible.

Lust unfolded deep inside my body like a lithe cat stretching its limbs. I could feel my body heating and beating with want, the little tingle of nerves, the flutter of my belly, the rush of my blood and the pounding of my heartbeat.

His gaze went to my mouth, stayed there for a pulsing moment, as if he was wondering if he could steal a kiss and get away with it. The thought thrilled me. The illicitness of it spoke to the wild woman in me I tried so desperately to keep contained.

I found myself stepping up on tippy-toes, leaning towards him, my mouth slightly parted in anticipation of the press of my lips to his.

'Oh, um, er, sorry,' Gracie said from the door.

I sprang back from Matt as if someone had fired a cannonball between us. Gracie was looking at me as if she had never seen me before. But then her eyes took on a wounded look, her pretty freckled face drooping in disappointment.

'It's not what you think—'

'I don't want to hear about it,' Gracie said crisply.

Matt straightened his tie, cleared his throat and moved past us both. 'I have patients to see,' he said, and left.

I closed my eyes for a second. My life was such a farce.

'Bertie, how *could* you?' Gracie said in a shocked voice.

'Nothing happened,' I said. 'We were just…talking.'

'I saw you lean towards him,' she said. 'What's *wrong* with you? You've just come back from your honeymoon, for God's sake. I never would've taken *you* for a player.'

'Who's being a player?' Jill asked, as she came breezing in with a stack of paperwork. She looked between Gracie and me and raised her artfully pencilled brows. 'You're not talking about Matt Bishop, are you? The man's entitled to have a private life, you know. Mind you, I'd give my back teeth to know whom he's seeing. No one seems to know but I'm sure it's someone from the hospital.'

I mentally rolled my eyes. Could this get any more ridiculously entangled?

'I believe he has a thing for married women,' Gracie said, shooting me a hard look.

Jill gave a disbelieving cough of laughter as she rolled back her chair to sit down. 'Can't see him following in his old man's footsteps.'

'What do you know about his father?' I asked.

Jill swivelled her chair to face me. 'Richard Bishop's a well-known womaniser, the younger the better, apparently. His wife Alexis turns a blind eye, has been doing so ever since their other son died.'

My insides lurched. 'What other son?'

'Matt's brother.'

I could feel my eyes popping. 'He has...*had* a brother?'

Jill gave me an odd look. 'Lots of people have siblings, Bertie.'

I brushed her comment aside with an impatient wave

of my hand. 'I know that, it's just he told me he was an only child.'

'Well, he is now,' Jill said flatly. 'Tim died when Matt was fifteen. Tim was two years older. He had a rock-climbing accident. He was in a coma for over a year before they finally turned off the ventilator.'

'How did you find out all this?' I asked.

'My sister-in-law went to school with Alexis,' Jill said. 'They'd lost touch over the years but recently re-connected on Facebook. I mentioned we had a new boss and when my sister-in-law heard Matt's name she gave me the background.'

Gracie was still eyeing me as if I were Jezebel in-carnate but I was beyond caring about that right now. I was still trying to get my head around Matt's tragic background. The loss of his older brother, the long stint in ICU before Tim was finally allowed to die. Was that why Matt was so adamant patients' relatives should be told the truth straight up? Had his parents clung to hope for months and months on end because they hadn't been told—or hadn't taken in—the reality of their eldest son's irretrievable condition?

Gracie muttered something about changing a pa-tient's IV fluids and left.

'So, who do you think Matt's seeing?' Jill asked.

'I hardly see how it's anyone's business.'

She let out a little sigh. 'You're right. Hospital gossip is like a virulent virus. Once it starts you can't stop it.'

Tell me about it, I thought.

Jill looked up at me again. 'Speaking of which, I heard in the tearoom there's a twenty-four-hour bug doing the rounds. They're isolating the cardiac ward. I reckon we might be next. Don't come into work if you get it.'

Right then I wished I never had to come to work ever again.

Gracie was in the change room when I went in to get my things before leaving for the day. She was getting her bag out of the locker and turned as I came in. 'Well, I'll say one thing. As new brides go, you have far more reason than most to blush.' She slammed the locker door. 'And here I was thinking you were different. More fool me.'

'Gracie—'

'I suppose that's why you didn't want to show me the wedding photos,' went on. 'You didn't want to be reminded you were married while you're sleeping with another man.'

'I'm not sleeping with—'

'Do you know what it feels like to be cheated on? *Do you?*' Her eyes watered and her voice shook. 'It's the worst feeling in the world.'

I knew all right. I took a deep breath. 'I didn't show you the photos because there aren't any.'

Her forehead puckered. 'What do you mean? Did they get deleted or something? That happened to a friend of mine. The photographer accidentally deleted them. If it hadn't been for other people's phone cameras, there would've been no photos at all.'

'They weren't deleted,' I said. 'They weren't taken in the first place.'

Her eyes were as round as the top of the linen bin next to the washbasin. 'Why not?'

My shoulders went down on a sigh. 'The wedding was called off. Andy was having an affair. I found out the night before the ceremony. It'd been going on for months.'

'Oh, my God!' Gracie clasped her hands over her mouth.

'I walked in on him with one of my bridesmaids' sister,' I said. 'It was… Anyway, there wasn't a wedding.'

She dropped her hands and asked, 'But why didn't you say something? You sent a postcard saying what a wonderful time you were having. Why have you let everyone assume—'

'Because I'm stupid, that's why.' I sat down on one of the bench seats and looked at my feet. I was wearing my piglet socks. There was a hole in one of the toes from Freddy chewing them. I should have darned them but I hadn't found the time.

'But surely you could've told me?' Gracie sounded so hurt I could barely bring myself to look at her. 'I know we've only known each other a few months but I thought we were mates. I told you all my stuff. And yet you didn't say a word. What sort of friendship is that?'

'I know. You're right. But I was too embarrassed,' I said. 'I didn't want everyone to feel sorry for me. To pity me. Poor old Bertie, dumped the night before her big day. The day she's been planning ever since she was five years old.'

Gracie's eyes were almost popping now. '*He* dumped *you*?'

'Yeah.' I let out another despondent sigh. 'That's the most embarrassing thing. If he hadn't pulled the plug I probably would've gone through with it to keep up appearances. Sick, huh?'

Gracie took one of my cold hands in hers and clasped it warmly. 'It's not sick. It's completely understandable. All that money, all those guests, all that food and—'

'God, don't remind me,' I groaned. 'Lucky it wasn't a huge wedding. We travelled around so much as kids I don't have a lot of friends.'

'You have more than you realise, Bertie,' she said, giving my hand another squeeze.

I looked into her china-blue eyes and somehow managed a vestige of a smile. 'Thanks.'

Gracie chewed her lip for a moment. 'Sorry about what I said back in the office. But don't you think you should let people know? I mean, what about that thing I saw between you and—'

'You didn't see anything.' I stood and wrapped my arms around my body as if the temperature had dropped twenty degrees. 'I was the one at fault. He was just standing there. I don't know what came over me.'

'So you're not involved with him?'

'How can I be even if I wanted to?' I asked. 'He thinks I'm married.'

'Then you should tell him and everyone else you're not.'

I swung back to face her again. 'No. I can't. What will everyone think? You have to keep it a secret. Please, Gracie, don't tell anyone. Promise me?'

She gave me a worried look. 'I'm hopeless at keeping secrets. I always leak stuff. I can't help it. It comes spilling out.'

'You have to promise me, Gracie.' I was almost to the

point of begging. It was pathetic. I was even thinking
of offering her money. 'You can't tell anyone. No one
must know. No one. Do you hear me? No one.'

'But—'

'No one will be interested in my private life in a
month or two,' I said. 'You know how it is with everyone here. We're all so busy we hardly have time to chat
about what's going on in our home lives. After a couple
of months I'll tell everyone I'm separated or had the
marriage annulled or something.'

Gracie chomped on her lower lip again, her expression doubtful. 'But what if you want to date someone
else? Dr Bishop, for instance.'

I tried to laugh it off but I didn't sound convincing
even to my ears. 'He's not interested in me. Not in the
long term anyway. I'm too out there for him.'

'I've seen the way he looks at you,' Gracie said. 'And
he was the one who organised for Jason Ryder to be
transferred to your room that first day. It was a heck of
a job moving the ventilator but he insisted it be done.
Not only that, if anyone dares to make fun of your project he cuts them off quick smart.'

Something in my chest spilled like a cup of warm
treacle. It was the thing I found most attractive about
Matt. Although he had reservations about my project,
he still managed to keep an open mind. That, and the
fact he stood up for me. How could I not find that the
most appealing trait? For as long as I can remember I
had dreamed of a knight in shining armour. The sort of
man who would protect me, shelter me and support me
in everything I attempted to do. Someone who believed

in me, in my potential, who helped me reach it without hindering it with their own self-serving interests.

But wasn't I dreaming an impossible dream? I was twenty-seven years old. I'd already wasted a chunk of my life on a man who wasn't right for me. Could I risk squandering another period of my life with a man who had offered me nothing but a behind-closed-doors… what? A fling? He hadn't exactly been specific about the terms. 'We'd make an interesting pair,' sounded more like an experiment than a relationship. Was that how he saw me? As a test sample?

What if I failed?

I'd had a full day in Theatre the following day so didn't get to ICU until we had to transfer the last patient. None of the other cases needed high dependency care so they went straight to Recovery. Once I was finished with the transfer I went to Matt's office. The door was closed and I gave it a tentative knock. There was no response so I knocked louder.

'He's gone home.'

I jumped about a foot when Jill Carter spoke from behind me. 'Oh.'

'He left a couple of hours ago,' she said. 'He was in most of the night with Rosanne Finch, the leukaemia patient. I told him to go home. I told him he looked worse than some of our patients.'

I frowned. 'Is he unwell?'

'He wouldn't admit it but I reckon he's got the bug. Gives you a blinding headache and a fever for twenty-four hours, give or take nausea and vomiting.'

'Sounds like a heap of fun.'

Jill smiled wryly. 'At least our husbands have us to wait on them hand on foot. What's yours like as a patient? If he's anything like mine, you'd rather be at work.'

'That just about sums it up,' I said.

CHAPTER EIGHT

I FOUND MATT'S great-aunt's house without any trouble. I asked one of the neighbours who was walking by with an overweight labrador which house had a corgi called Winnie.

Here's what I've found out recently. Dog owners have their own network. It's like the medical community—everyone knows everyone. The only difference with dog owners is they only know the dogs' names, not each other's. They call each other things like Fifi's mum or Milo's dad. Weird but true.

The house was a lovely Victorian mansion—personally, I thought it was way too big for a single old lady—with a lovely knot garden at the front, which was currently covered in snow. There was a light on downstairs but the upper floors were dark. I pressed my finger to the brass doorbell and listened as it rang throughout the house. I heard Winnie bark and then the click-clack of her claws on the floor. After what seemed a long time I heard someone coming down the stairs. They weren't happy footsteps.

The door opened and Matt stood there dressed in nothing but a pair of drawstring cotton pyjama bottoms. I stared at his chest and abs. He was so cut it looked like he had stepped off a plinth in the Uffizi in Florence. My fingers itched to touch him, to trace my fingertips over every hard ridge and contour. I dragged my eyes up to his. His weren't pleased to see me, or at least that was the impression I got. 'I thought you might like some company,' I said.

'Now's not a good time.'

I looked at his forehead, where beads of perspiration had gathered. The rest of his features looked pale and drawn. 'Consider it a house call,' I said.

He managed to summon enough energy to lift one of his eyebrows but I could tell it caused pain somewhere inside his head by the way he winced. 'I thought you didn't make house calls?'

I pushed past him in the door. 'I'm making an exception.' I bent down to ruffle Winnie's ears. 'Besides, this old girl could do with a walk, surely?'

'It won't hurt her to miss a day.'

I turned back to face him. 'Stop frowning at me like that. It'll make your headache worse.'

'How do you know I have a headache?'

I gave him a look. 'Have you taken something for it?'

He dragged a hand down his face, wincing again. 'Paracetamol.'

'You probably need something stronger.'

'What I need is to be left alone.'

I put my hands on my hips. Jem calls it my 'taking-charge pose'. I can be quite bossy when I put my mind to it. 'Come on, off to bed with you. I'll sort out the dog and rustle up something for you to eat and drink.'

He made a groaning noise. 'Don't mention that word in my hearing.'

'When was the last time you ate?'

He gave me a glare but it didn't really have any sting in it. 'Yesterday.'

I shifted my lips from side to side. 'Fluids?'

'A couple of sips of water.'

'When?'

He let out an exhausted-sounding breath. 'You don't give up easily, do you?'

'I've been playing doctors and nurses since I was three,' I said. 'Now, where is your bedroom?'

He scored his fingers through the tousled thickness of his hair. 'Second floor. First on the right.'

I made my way to the kitchen and boiled the kettle and made a cup of chamomile tea, which is really good for settling an upset stomach. I had brought herbal tea bags with me as I know from experience that not everyone has them in their pantry. I was right about Matt's aunt. She only had English Breakfast and Lady Grey. I took the steaming cup up on a gorgeous silver tray I found in a display cabinet and carried it upstairs. I felt like one of the chambermaids in *Downton Abbey*.

Matt was lying in a tangle of sweaty sheets, his forearm raised at a right angle over his eyes. I got a good look at his chest and abdomen. Ripped muscles, just like an old-fashioned washboard, lean and toned with just a nice sprinkling of chest hair that fanned from his pectoral muscles into a V below the drawstring waist of his pyjama bottoms.

I hadn't realised how sexy male pyjamas could be, way more sexy than sleeping naked. It was the thought of what was hiding behind that thin layer of cotton that so tantalised me. He was lying with his legs slightly apart, his feet and ankles turned outwards, his stomach not just flat but hollowed in like a shallow cave. I looked at it in unmitigated envy. My stomach was more dome-like than the one on St Paul's Cathedral. I sucked it in and approached the bed. 'I have a cup of tea for you.'

He cranked open one eye. 'You don't have to do this.'

'Here.' I held the cup up to his mouth. 'Just take a few sips. It'll help with the nausea.'

He raised his head off the pillow and took a small sip but then he sprayed it out as if it were poison. 'What the freaking hell is that?'

'Chamomile tea,' I said.

He gave me a black look. 'It tastes like stewed grass clippings.'

I put the cup on the bedside table and mopped the front of my jumper with a tissue I'd plucked from the box near the bed. 'You won't feel better until you get some fluids on board. Maybe I should bring an IV set from the hospital and run a couple of litres into you.'

'Don't even think about it.'

I got up from the edge of the bed and went through to the ensuite bathroom. It was a beautiful affair, with black and white tiles on the floor and a freestanding white bath with brass clawed feet. The shower was separate and had brass fittings the same as the bath taps. There were black and white towels hanging on a brass rail, although there were another couple on the floor next to the shower, as if Matt hadn't had the energy to pick them up after he'd showered.

There was shaving gear on the marble counter where

the washbasin was situated and one of those shaving mirrors, the one with one side magnified. I absolutely loathe them as they always show up my chicken-pox scar above my left eye. You guessed it. My parents went through an anti-vaccination phase.

I ran the tap to dampen a facecloth. I wrung it out and sprinkled a couple of drops of lavender oil, which I'd brought with me, on it and took it back to the bedroom.

Matt was still lying in that body-fallen-from-a-tall-building pose. I swear I could have drawn a chalk line around him like in one of those film noir murder mysteries. I gently pulled his arm away from his eyes and laid the facecloth over them. He gave a deep sigh, which made his whole body relax into the mattress.

'Did you hear that?' he said.

'What? Your sigh?'

'That hiss of steam.'

I laughed. 'You certainly are running a fever. Do you have a thermometer anywhere?'

'I have a doctor's bag in the study downstairs.'

I got up from the bed. 'I'll be back in a tick.'

I was at the door when his voice stopped me in my tracks. 'Bertie?'

I turned and looked at him. 'Yes?'

He opened his mouth to say something but then he closed it. 'Doesn't matter.'

'No, go on, tell me.'

He looked at me for a beat or two. 'Why did you come here tonight?'

I pulled at my lower lip with my teeth, not quite able to hold his gaze. I'm not sure I knew exactly why I'd come myself. I had acted on automatic, as if it had been programmed for me to walk the block that separated our places of residence and call on him. 'I know what it's like to come home to an empty house when you're feeling rotten.'

There was a little pulse of silence. I was feeling pretty proud of myself for not trying to fill it.

He closed his eyes. 'Forget about the thermometer. I need to sleep.'

'If you're sure.'

'I'm sure.'

I left him upstairs sleeping and took Winnie out for a walk. I found a spare key on the hall table so I didn't get locked out. Matt looked so exhausted I thought he might not hear me on my return. Winnie and I didn't go far as it was freezing but she seemed to enjoy the outing. She stopped at just about every lamppost for a sniff and a minuscule pee, before trotting on to the next one and doing it all over again. *That is quite some pelvic floor she has*, I thought.

I took her back and fed her and then had a good old snoop around. I love looking at other people's houses. I get lots of ideas for decorating my own. Well, that's my rationalisation anyway. Matt's great-aunt had excellent taste and clearly money was no object. The place was decked out in the most luxurious soft furnishings and the furniture was mostly antique, and not just charity-shop antiques either. I mean *real* antiques, like centuries-old pieces that were heirlooms that looked like they should be in the Victoria and Albert museum.

But it wasn't a house I could imagine a young family

growing up in. I began to wonder what sort of house Matt had spent his childhood in. Was it like this one, a showpiece of wealth but without the warmth and heart of a house where children's laughter was always welcome? I wondered too about his older brother. Whether they were close and how Tim's death had impacted on him.

Was that why he was so driven and focussed on work? His blunt honesty about a patient's prognosis made a lot of sense now I knew his brother had spent so long in ICU before he finally died. I had seen enough relatives do the long stints in the unit, watching for any sign of change, their hopes hanging in the air like fragile threads that could be destroyed with a look or ill-timed word from a doctor.

That final walk from the unit once a loved one has passed away is one of the saddest things to watch. Some people hold themselves together, walking tall and straight, or putting their arms around other family members, keeping strong for the rest of the family. Others cry and wail and scream in denial and some have to be physically escorted, as they can't bear to bring themselves to leave. Others look for scapegoats, lashing out at staff or other relatives, apportioning blame as a way of dealing with overwhelming grief.

I wondered how Matt had handled his older brother's death. Had he stood tall and quiet and dignified or had he railed and ranted against the injustice of a young life cut short? Or had he buried his grief so deeply it rarely got an airing?

He was a complex man, caring and considerate, strong and capable and disciplined, but with a sense of humour that countered his rather formal, take-no-prisoners demeanour. I wondered if he would have turned out a different, more open and friendly person if his brother hadn't died. His real self was locked away behind layers of grief, only getting an airing when he felt safe enough to let his guard down.

I suddenly wished I were that person. The person he would open up to in a way he had never done with anyone else. Hadn't he already let me in a tiny bit? He had mentioned all had not been well with his childhood. He had mentioned his father and mother's relationship. Would he eventually tell me more, reveal more of the man he truly was? I hoped so. I had a sense we could be allies. Our childhoods couldn't have been more different but there was an air of loneliness…of otherness about him I could definitely relate to.

I found Matt's doctor's bag in the study downstairs. It was a beautiful room kitted up like an English country estate library. There were wall-to-ceiling bookshelves and there was even one of those extendable ladder-like steps to reach the top shelves. There was an antique desk with a Louis IV chair and an old world globe. The only modern thing in the room, apart from the electricity and Matt's doctor's bag, was a laptop on the desk. I admit I like a little snoop from time to time but I draw the line at reading other people's emails. Matt's computer was in sleep mode in any case, but there was a part of me that dearly would have liked to know if he'd mentioned me to any of his friends.

But then I saw a handwritten note lying on the desk next to an old inkwell and quill. My reading speed was faster than my moral rectitude. I was halfway down the page before I realised I was reading something that was meant to be private, but by then it was too late.

Matthew,
It's your father's birthday next month. I know you're not speaking to him after the last time you visited but he didn't mean it. He'd had too much red wine. You know he can never remember what he's said the next morning.

Anyway, I know you're busy but it would be lovely if you'd pop in. You don't have to stay long. I'm not doing anything too big. Just having a few friends around for cocktails. I wouldn't want Eleanor Grantonberry next door to think I couldn't put on a proper do for my husband.

Feel free to bring a date. Are you seeing anyone? You never tell me anything! Isn't it time you got over Helena? She wasn't right for you. You're too much of a workaholic. She and Simon are very happy. Did you know she's pregnant? The baby's due in June. I wish you could find a nice girl to settle down and have babies with.

Love Mum x

I sat on the chair and looked at that piece of paper for a long time. I wished my mum were there to do a hand-writing analysis. But I could pick up enough between the lines to realise Matt had a complicated background.

And here I was, thinking mine was a little weird.

I went back upstairs with some chicken broth I'd made while Matt slept. I'd found some ingredients in the pantry and fridge and freezer and whipped up my classic cure-all. I set it out on a tray with a starched doily I'd found and carried it upstairs.

Matt opened his eyes as I came in. 'You're still here?'

'I haven't got anything on this evening.' I set the tray on the bedside table. 'Do you think you could manage a bit of broth once I take your temp?'

'Did you make it?'

'Don't worry, it's not laced with poison.'

He frowned. 'Sorry, I didn't mean to sound—'

'I did, however, sprinkle some eye of newt in it.'

He smiled a crooked smile. 'Don't make me laugh. It makes my head hurt.'

'Poor baby.'

I popped the thermometer in his mouth and waited for it to beep. I took it out and looked at the reading. 'Hmm, it's back to normal. The rest must've done the trick.'

I sat beside him on the bed as he worked his way through the bowl of broth. He didn't manage it all but he seemed to enjoy what he had. He even had a glass of mineral water with a squeeze of lemon I'd brought up.

Once he was finished I got up to take the tray back down to the kitchen. 'Why don't you have a shower and I'll sort out your bed for you? I'll even do hospital corners.'

He frowned again. 'Seriously, Bertie, you don't have to do this.'

'I know, but I want to.'

His eyes looked into mine. 'Why?'

'Everyone needs a friend now and again.'

His frown deepened as his eyes moved away from

mine. 'I'm not sure I'm the sort of friend you need right now.'

'Because you haven't got over H-her?' I caught myself just in time. I didn't want him to know I'd been reading his private mail, although he might put two and two together once he realised I'd been in the study to get his doctor's bag. I'd left everything as I'd found it, but if he knew anything about women at all, he must know I would have read it.

He let out a long, uneven breath. 'I'm not good at relationships, any relationships. I hurt and disappoint people without even trying.'

'So you keep things casual with anyone who comes along who interests you.'

He gave me a measured look. 'Is that how you see us? As something casual?'

I wasn't sure how to answer. What exactly was he offering? Come to that, what was *I* offering? I couldn't hope to hide my attraction to him. My body had its own silent language. I could feel it calling out to him even then. The tightening of my core, the flush running over my skin, the way my eyes kept going from his to his mouth and back again. The way my tongue moistened my lips. Even the way I'd turned up tonight, playing nursemaid, surely told him all he needed to know. But how could I have what I wanted without causing even more mayhem in my life?

His eyes had a dark glint in them. 'I can see how it's risky, given your...situation.'

My teeth sank into my lip. Here was my chance to confess what a fool I'd been. The words were assembled on my tongue like paratroopers about to leave a Hercules aircraft. I knew once I let them out I couldn't take them back. How soon before he would tell someone at work about my game of charades? But there was no way I could allow him to make love to me while he thought I was married. 'There's something I have to tell you... I should've told you earlier.'

'I know.'

I kept talking, barely registering he had even spoken. Now that I'd made up my mind to confess I had to get on with it without distraction. I had to get it out there before he kissed me or I lost my courage. Not that I'd had much to begin with. 'I've been lying to you about my...situation,' I said. 'There was no wedding. I was jilted the night before. I was too embarrassed to tell anyone. I went on my honeymoon alone and I stupidly wrote a couple of postcards when I was tipsy, pretending everything had gone ahead as planned.' I shook my head at my own foolishness, not wanting to look at Matt in case I saw the derision I was sure he must feel. 'Postcards. Can you believe it? Who writes postcards these days? How *dumb* is that?'

'I know.'

'But the thing is I never intended to post them,' I said, without even acknowledging Matt's calm insertion. 'The housekeeping staff took them when I was out of the room and kindly posted them for me. I should've known something like that would happen.' I took a breath and went on, 'I seem to always get myself into ridiculous situations. And then when I came back to work that first day there was my stupid postcard on the noticeboard. If I'd been sensible I would've phoned or emailed ahead or something. But walking in like that to their smiling faces, I...I just couldn't do it. How could I tell them that...?'

Somewhere in the workings of my fevered brain I finally registered what he'd just said. Twice. I looked at him with a quizzical expression. 'You know what?'

His eyes had that spark of amusement shining in them again. 'I know you're not married.'

I gaped at him with my mouth so wide open you could have backed a London bus into it. *'You know?'*

His smile had a teasing element to it that made my blood start to tick with anger. 'I knew from the start.'

He knew?

A red mist came up in front of my eyes.

He'd known from the start?

My veins were so bloated with anger they felt like they were going to combust. It was rocketing through my body like a cruise missile. He'd known and not told me? Not given me a single hint?

Why?

I clamped my lips together to force myself to think before I spoke. But I was too upset to think. My thoughts were tumbling around my head like a handful of marbles in a glass bowl. It physically hurt to try and make sense of them. Had he been laughing at me behind all his casually posed questions? Questions about my 'husband' and where I went on my honeymoon. *Grrr!* He'd known the *whole time* how awkward I would find those questions and yet he had continued each time we interacted as if I were a new bride. What had motivated him? Had he *enjoyed* my discomfiture, my wretched squirming every time we spoke?

Of course he had. He'd led me on, teasing me, mocking me with his enigmatic looks and half-smiles. The crushing hurt was worse than my anger. It pressed down on my sternum like a chest of drawers. He had deliberately led me on—for what? To have a joke at my expense? So he could laugh about me with all my colleagues?

'How did you know?' I fired the question at him like a round of bullets. 'How could you possibly know? No one at the hospital knows, apart from Gracie McCurcher, and she's sworn to secrecy.'

He was still looking at me with an amused expression, which wasn't doing my escalating anger any favours. I felt like a pressure cooker inside me was about to explode. I could feel it expanding in my chest until I could scarcely draw breath.

'I heard about it via an old school friend of mine who works in the same company as your ex,' he said. 'We met for a drink a couple of days before you returned to work. He told me how he'd just come back from Yorkshire where the wedding of his colleague had been cancelled at the last minute. I wouldn't have taken any notice except he mentioned your name. *Bertie* is quite unusual so when you turned up at work I put two and two together.'

I gave him a livid glare. 'So why didn't you blow my cover then and there? That would've been quite a laugh for you, along with my project title.'

The amused look was exchanged for one that suspiciously looked like pity, or at least something very close to it. 'I figured you had your reasons for keeping quiet about it. I decided to play along for a bit.'

I sent him another paint-stripping look. Seriously, I

could've taken my new paint burner back to the hardware store and used my gaze on my house instead. 'Why?' I shot back. 'So you could have a joke at my expense? Mock me while you pretended to be interested in me?'

His eyes darkened to a deeper bluey grey as they held mine, his voice deep and gravelly. 'I wasn't pretending.'

My heart kicked against my breastbone. 'You weren't?'

He shook his head.

'Oh, well, then…'

'You have to tell everyone, Bertie. Surely you see that?'

I stood from the bed and crossed my arms over my body. 'No. No. No. I can't. I just can't.'

'Why are you so worried about what people will say?'

I turned back to look at him. 'I spent most of my childhood being laughed at. I can't bear people sniggering at me, or—worse—pitying me. If I were to tell everyone now I was jilted the night before my wedding they'll howl with laughter or cringe in pity. It's too late. I have to keep it quiet. I *have* to.'

'Come here.' His voice had a commanding tone to it I found wonderfully soothing. It was like he was going to take charge—please, don't tell my bra-burning mother I said that!—and make everything right for me. I sat beside him on the bed and he took one of my hands in his. 'You don't have to keep pretending. The longer it goes on the harder it'll be to undo. People will understand. They really will, sweetheart. Trust me.'

It really got me when he called me that. A lot of men utter endearments without making them sound genuine.

But I wasn't convinced a tell-all in the staffroom was going to work for me. Besides, I didn't have the guts to do it. My childhood scars were too deep, too raw to have them scraped open by even one giggle or chuckle. 'Please,' I said. 'Please, try and understand.'

He gave my hand a gentle squeeze, his eyes holding mine in a tender look. I don't think anyone—no man at least—has ever looked at me like that. He looked like he really cared about me, about my feelings, about my insecurities. 'I do understand. It's tough when things don't work out the way you'd planned. But you'll get over it in time.'

I gave him a narrowed look. 'Please, don't tell me you feel sorry for me.'

He stroked his thumb over the back of my hand. 'I feel sorry you feel so pressured to fit in that you can't be honest with people. But you don't have to hide or pretend with me, okay?'

I could feel a little wobble of my chin, which was the closest I've got to crying in a very long time. 'Okay.' It was barely a whisper but it sure felt good to say it. To admit I trusted him to keep my secret safe.

He trailed a finger over the back of my hand. 'There's a way around this.'

I suppressed a shiver as his finger travelled to the underside of my wrist where my pulse was skyrocketing. 'There is?'

His eyes scorched mine. 'We could have a secret relationship.'

I noted the word 'secret'. Not my favourite word right then, but still. I swallowed as his finger made a lazy circle against the skin of my palm. It felt like he had touched me intimately, stroking me to arousal. 'I want you to know I don't do this sort of thing normally.'

'I know.'

I looked at him again. Directly. Staunchly. 'I mean it, Matt. This is totally out of character for me.'

He gently brushed a strand of hair back from my face. I had always longed for a man to do that to me. Andy never seemed to notice my tendrils, even the ones I'd deliberately staged to hang loose so he could push them back. 'Maybe we need to get this thing between us out of our system. What do you say?'

'Well,' I said, tapping my finger against my lip for a moment, 'I do have a couple of stipulations.'

'Which are?'

'This bed, for one thing.' I stood up and put my hands on my hips again. 'If I'm going to have bed-wrecking sex with you, then we at least need to start with a bed that's not already wrecked.'

He gave another lopsided smiled as he swung his legs over the side of the bed. 'You are one crazy girl.'

'But you like me, right?'

He stood and brushed his fingertips down my cheek, his smile, even as it faded, still making my insides turn over. 'I hope you don't catch my bug.'

'Thanks to my parents, I have a robust immune system.'

He gave one of my Dorothy from Oz pigtails a gentle tug. 'You're going to need it.'

CHAPTER NINE

I REMADE THE bed with fresh linen and dumped the other in the laundry downstairs. I would have set on a load but I had other priorities right then. When I came back up Matt was standing next to the bed with just a towel draped around his hips. I went to him as if I'd been doing it all my adult life. It felt so natural to walk into his open arms and feel them come around me like strong, warm bands.

He smelt divine, soap and shampoo and his own male smell, and he was warm and still a little damp from the shower. I was damp too. I could feel my body stirring in response to his closeness; the maleness of him against my softer contours was enough to send my senses spinning.

His mouth came down to the side of mine, touching and teasing the corner of my mouth in a tantalisingly little prelude of what was to come. I turned my head so his lips came into full contact with mine. I wasn't in the mood for preludes. I wanted the whole damn symphony and in forte.

His mouth was warm and firm and moved against mine with devastating expertise. There was amazing choreography in our kisses. There were no nose bumps or tooth scrapes; instead, there was a natural affinity between our mouths, a graceful coordination like watching two brilliant dancers working the ballroom floor. My response to him was purely instinctive. I hadn't even thought I was a particularly good kisser until I had come into contact with his mouth.

His tongue stroked along my bottom lip and I made a sound of approval as I welcomed him inside. The warm glide of his tongue over and under and around mine made my insides contract with lust. His hands pulled me against him, his fingers digging into my buttocks to hold me against where his blood pounded with desire. I could feel the hard ridge of him swelling against me. It made my body restless to get even closer. I could feel the tingling and tickling of my inner core, an ache and pulse of longing growing more intense by the second.

His hands began working their way under my jumper, sliding his palms over my bare skin to find my breast. I made a little gasping sound as his fingers pushed aside my bra and made flesh-to-flesh contact. He cupped me first, and then he rolled the pad of his thumb back and forth across and around my nipple. It was the most exquisite torture. All the nerves beneath my skin leapt and twirled and pirouetted.

I wanted to touch him to give him the same pleasure he was giving me. I tugged at the towel covering him and it fell to the floor. I stroked my fingers down his hard, flat abdomen, stringing out the anticipation for him as I slowly made my way to my target. He sucked in a harsh-sounding breath as I claimed my prize. He was iron hard and yet his skin felt velvet smooth. I felt the throbbing pulse of his blood against my hand. I squeezed and stroked in turn. I circled my fingertip over his tip, where pre-ejaculate fluid was beading. It was an erotic reminder of the primal impulses going on in my own body, the silky dew that moistened my inner walls in preparation for the thrust and glide of his body.

He helped me out of my clothes with gentle but urgent hands, using those same hands to stroke over my flesh as he uncovered it. I felt like a present he was unwrapping, a present he had waited a long time to claim. He kissed every inch of my décolletage, along the scaffold of my collarbones, dipping his tongue into the suprasternal notch between.

His mouth came back to mine, plundering it with increasing vigour, as if the tight hold on his self-control was under enormous strain. I kissed him back with passionate enthusiasm, my tongue dancing and duelling with his. He tasted so fresh, a combination of mint and salt and sexy maleness. He had shaved during his shower but his skin still rasped against mine in a way that made me feel incredibly feminine.

Once I was in nothing but my knickers, his hands came up and cupped my face. I liked it that he hadn't stripped me naked, that he'd allowed me that final barrier to make me feel less pressured, less exposed. I could still feel him against me, the hot probe of his erection making my body ache behind the lace of my underwear.

His lifted his mouth off mine so our lips were almost touching, our breaths mingling in the intimate space. 'Are you sure about this?' he said.

That was another thing I liked. He hadn't taken my consent for granted. He'd allowed me time to back out if

I wasn't comfortable with taking things further. I don't want to make Andy sound like a predator or anything but there were a few times when he hadn't really picked up on my change of mind or mood.

'I'm sure.' I put my hand to his face and stroked it down the chiselled plane of his jaw. 'But thanks for asking.'

He rested his forehead against mine. 'It's been a while for me.'

'Me too.'

He lifted his head to look at me. 'How long?'

'It's been a couple of months.' I gave him a wry look. 'Actually, it's probably longer.'

He brushed his lips against mine. 'Good girl.'

'Why'd you say that?'

He smiled at me. 'You're being honest.'

The words I was going to say were obliterated in the combustible heat of our mouths meeting in a scorching hot kiss that spoke of the deep, irresistible yearnings going on in both of our bodies. Our tongues tangled and teased, stroked and swept and chased each other in a sensual dance as sexy as any Latin tango.

I was standing up on tiptoe, my breasts pushed almost flat against his chest in an effort to get as close as possible. His hands gently peeled away my knickers; his palms warm as they cupped my bare behind. He moved against me, the strong pulse of his body sending mine into a frenzy of want.

He pulled back from me slightly. 'I need to get a condom.'

He left me briefly to find one in his wallet. He didn't have a supply in the bedside drawer, I noticed, which seemed to suggest he hadn't brought anyone back here before. I liked the special feeling it gave me, the feeling that I was the only woman he'd considered making love with since he'd got back from the States.

He came back to me sheathed and gently guided me to the bed, where we ended up in an erotic tangle of limbs. That was another thing I noticed. There was no awkwardness about who was going to put which limb where. We fitted together like one of those complicated puzzles that only a Mensa member can solve. The feel of his naked skin moving against mine, the glide and stroke of his hands, the caress of his lips and tongue and the heat of our connection went through every pore of my body like a current.

I stroked my hands over his back and shoulders, discovering every knob of his vertebrae as his mouth savoured mine. Our tongues did that sexy little tango again that mimicked what our lower bodies were aching and straining to do. I shifted beneath him, urging him to take things to the next stage, but he was taking his time to ensure I was properly aroused. He stroked my entrance, felt the wetness of me and then slid one finger inside. I almost came right then and there. He stroked his fingertip across my clitoris, just enough to make me aware of him.

The sensations gathered like an approaching wave, building momentum with a force that threatened to overwhelm me. I felt the tension building in my body as he stroked me again, softly, slowly, then varying the speed, getting to know what I liked and what I didn't.

Just when I thought I couldn't take any more he moved down my body, kissing my breasts, down my sternum to my belly button and then to the top of my mons pubis. Instead of using his fingers, this time he used his lips and tongue. I know I sound like a ridiculous prude but I've never really understood all the fuss about oral sex. Andy did his best, but I always felt he couldn't wait to get it over with so he could get on with the main event, so to speak. I would freeze up or fret that I hadn't waxed or that I might not be as fresh as I should be down there. I would end up pretending I'd had a good time just to get it over with.

But with Matt I forgot about all those insecurities and hang-ups. His caresses were so perfectly timed, so cleverly orchestrated my body went on a feverish journey of discovery that left me completely breathless. The orgasm rolled over me like a massive wave, spinning and tossing me into a world of sensation that left no room for conscious thought. I was reduced to that one part of my body, my most primal part. I writhed and clawed and cried and gasped as the ricocheting pulses went through me, finally leaving me in a limp heap as the afterglow flowed through every muscle in my body.

Matt came back over me, cradling the side of my face with one of his hands. He didn't ask if it was good for me. He didn't need to. Instead, he kissed me again, the taste of my own body on his lips stirring me into a new round of arousal.

I reached for him to guide him into my body but he really didn't need any help from me. He knew exactly where he was going. But he didn't thrust in hard, not at first. He took his time, inching in to allow me to get used to his length. I felt like a virgin having sex for the first time with someone who really knew what they were doing. I felt special and respected and worshiped, instead of exploited and used.

Once he sensed my body was fine with him being fully enclosed, he began to move. It's a rhythm as old as time but each couple has their own take on it. I never found my groove with Andy, or my other partners. I always felt I was three steps behind, like a novice dancer trying to join a complicated line dance. I was always out of sequence, out of time with my partners.

But with Matt I felt everything fall into place. He moved and I responded. Our bodies rocked together as if they had been programmed to do it. When he groaned with deep pleasure it made my flesh shiver all over. But instead of taking his pleasure, he hadn't finished giving me mine. He somehow got his hand between our bodies and found my clitoris again and stroked and coaxed it into an earth-shattering orgasm. It was so powerful I could feel it rippling through me, the tight contractions triggering his release. I felt the deep shudder of his body as it drove into mine in those last desperate pumps as he emptied. I felt his skin lift in goose bumps and stroked my hands over his back and shoulders and down over his lower spine and taut buttocks.

Neither of us spoke.

I didn't want to break the mood with banal conversation. I wanted to dwell in that quiet sense of physical harmony, the soothing mutual relaxation of two bodies that moments ago had been strung tight with sexual tension but which had now found peace.

It was a while before I realised Matt was soundly asleep. I know a lot a men fall asleep after sex, but at least he hadn't rolled away to the other side of the bed and started snoring like a wild boar.

He had quietly slipped into a deep and relaxing slumber while still holding me in his arms. For some strange reason I felt like crying. Not because he hadn't stayed awake long enough to tell me I was the best sex partner he'd ever had—as if *that* was going to happen—but because he felt comfortable enough with me to truly relax. I got the feeling he didn't do it too often.

After half an hour or so I gently extricated myself from his hold. He made a soft, deep murmur of something that sounded a little like protest but he didn't fully wake up. I covered him with the quilt and tiptoed about the room to collect my clothes. I dressed in the bathroom, and then, once I had restored some sense of order to my hair, I went downstairs. I gave Winnie a last pat and made sure she had doggy biscuits and a fresh bowl of water, and then I let myself out.

CHAPTER TEN

I HAD A pre-assessment clinic first thing the next day and then a meeting with the other anaesthetists about some minor changes to the training scheme. Then I had a list in Theatre that went over time due to the weirdest case of appendicitis I've ever seen, or the surgeon for that matter. Despite the patient only being seventeen, the appendix had been massively expanded and completely replaced by what looked like a tumour.

It meant I was nowhere near ICU until quite late in the day. I hadn't seen or spoken to Matt since I'd left his place the night before, but I knew he was at work because I'd overheard two of the theatre nurses talking about him.

'I walked past Matt Bishop on my way to work this morning,' Leanne said. 'Talk about hot. Do you know who he's seeing?'

'No, but I wish it was me,' the other one, called Kathy, said in a tone that suggested she was waggling her eyebrows.

I tried not to eavesdrop but my ears were out on cornstalks.

The girls must have sensed my interest as they turned

to me, where I was tidying up my equipment. 'Who do you think it is, Bertie?'

'Why would you think I would know?' I sounded a bit defensive. Way too defensive.

'Someone said he's seeing a married woman and she works at St Iggy's,' Kathy said.

'That's just malicious gossip and you shouldn't be spreading it,' I said. I immediately regretted it. I saw the way their eyebrows went up in unison.

'Touchy,' Leanne said.

'Anyway,' Kathy pitched in, 'why would you be so worried about what's said about him? Isn't he going to pull the plug on your research?'

I tried to keep my composure cool and indifferent but I could feel a hot tide of colour sweeping up from my neck to my face. 'Not if I can produce results.'

'You'd better watch out, Bertie,' Leanne said. 'If it's true Dr Bishop has a thing for married women, you might be his next target.'

'That's ridiculous,' I said. 'I'm not—'

'Interested?' Kathy said. 'Come on, you might've just got back from your honeymoon but you wouldn't be human if you didn't find him attractive.'

I could have told them then and there. *I'm not married.* But I could just imagine the fallout. The news would spread like wildfire. I would be the topic of every locker room and staff tearoom conversation. Everywhere I went people would give me those looks, the looks I'd faced for most of my twenty-seven years. Pity. Ridicule. Mockery.

Just as well I got a call about a patient in Recovery. I made good my escape and left.

* * *

I went to ICU after I finished in Recovery to check on
Jason. His wife, Megan, was there, his parents having
gone home after spending most of the day with him.
She looked exhausted so I sat with her for a while, just
listening as she told me about the plans she and Jason
had made. Their excitement over finding they were to
become parents, how they had chosen names and decided against finding out the sex of the baby, as they
wanted the thrill of the surprise.

She even showed me the ultrasound images. Seeing
a baby in utero in 3D stirred my own maternal long-
ings in my body. I had squashed them down for years as
I'd concentrated on my career, but now, as I got closer
and closer to the big three-oh, I was hearing some very
loud ticking.

Andy hadn't been so keen on having kids straight
away but, like a lot of women, I'd assumed he'd change
his mind once we were married. It was only when I
saw him with that girl that I realised he wasn't mature
enough to be a father. He was too selfish to want to
give up his freedom and take responsibility for someone other than himself.

I berated myself for being so blind about him. I had
let the years roll on, reassuring myself things would
get better when they had got progressively worse. Why
hadn't I acknowledged it? Why had I let it get to the
night before the wedding to see my relationship with
him for what it was?

Once I was sure Megan was comfortable with a fresh
glass of juice and some sandwiches from the doctors'
room—I was bending the rules, but the ones in the

relatives' room weren't as nice, in my opinion—I left the unit.

Matt was coming out of his office as I was coming along the corridor to leave for the day. I'd thought of nothing else but him ever since I'd left his great-aunt's house the night before. I wanted to see him again. I wanted to explore the amazing chemistry we had together. My body was still aware of him. It still tingled every time I thought of the passion we had shared.

He stopped in the process of closing his door, pushing it open instead and indicating with his head for me to come inside. 'Got a minute?'

I walked past him in the doorway, my body zinging with awareness as one of his shirtsleeves brushed me on the way past. I turned and faced him once he'd closed the door. It was hard to read his expression. I wondered if he was regretting last night. I wasn't his usual type. But, then, I wasn't anyone's usual type. Maybe he was regretting making love to me now he was over his bug. Maybe I'd caught him at a weak moment. Maybe he didn't even like me. See how insecure I am? It's ridiculous.

'How are you feeling?' I asked lightly.

'Good. You?'

'Great. Fine. Peachy.' I always go overboard when I'm feeling nervous. I wasn't sure how to handle the morning-after routine, especially in the context of our relationship. I wasn't even sure what the context was. I couldn't have a proper relationship with him while I was pretending to be married, but what was he offering if I came clean? Hadn't he said he wasn't interested in

anything lasting? He was too busy with other priorities
or some other get-out clause he'd used.

He leaned back against his desk in his usual manner. 'That was the best chicken broth I've had in a long
while, perhaps ever.'

'It's my own secret recipe.'

'I could tell.'

I wasn't sure we were talking about chicken broth,
especially the way he was looking at me. I tried not
to blush but all I could think about was how his body
had felt inside mine. 'So…what did you want to see
me about?'

'I suppose you've heard the gossip?'

I chewed at my mouth. 'Yes.'

'Any more thoughts on coming clean?'

I crossed my arms over my body. 'No.'

His eyebrows drew together. 'Even after last night?'

I affected a casual look, as if I had amazing, mind-
blowing sex with men all the time. 'Why after last
night?'

He looked at me in a frowning way. But then he
closed off his expression. The screen came up and I
was locked out. Something pinched inside my stomach. 'So you're still determined to run with this crazy
charade,' he said.

I sent him an intractable look. 'I'm not ready to have
my private life the subject of everyone's amusement.'

His brow furrowed back into a deep frown. 'Do you
really think people will find it funny that you were
jilted?'

I jerked up my chin. '*You* obviously did. Stringing

me along for three flipping weeks, asking all those stupid husband and honeymoon questions.'

He let out a whooshing breath. 'I suppose I deserve that.' He scraped a hand through his hair again, before dropping his hand back down by his side. 'Look, I wasn't really laughing at you. I was amused by the lengths you were going to when all you had to do was tell everyone the truth. People go through break-ups all the time. Relationships either work or they don't.'

I glared at him again. How absolutely typical to dismiss the emotional turmoil of what a break-up like mine had entailed. Easy come, easy go was obviously his credo. Well, it certainly wasn't mine. I was the one who'd had to face all those guests. I was the one who'd had to endure all those looks of abject pity. I was the one who was still trying to pick up the pieces of my life.

'I was twelve hours away from my wedding,' I said. 'The wedding day I'd been planning since I was a little girl. I'd been going out with Andy for five and a half years. We'd been engaged for eighteen months. That's a little different from being dumped after a lousy date or two.'

His expression stilled with seriousness. 'I know how hard a break-up is. But it's not as if you were in love with him.'

My eyes rounded in affront. 'Oh, and you're suddenly an expert on *my* feelings, are you? What gives you the right to say such a ridiculous thing? Of course I loved him. I was going to marry him, wasn't I?'

The look he gave me reminded me of the look a disappointed parent gives to a wilfully disobedient child.

It made me angrier than I had any right to be. He had touched on a nerve that was still a little sensitive.

But I wasn't prepared to admit just how sensitive.

'If you were still in love with him you would never have come to my place last night,' he said. 'You must've known what would happen between us, or are you lying to yourself now as well as everyone else?'

Of course he was right. I would never have slept with him if I'd had feelings for another man. But I was confused about my feelings for Matt. They were a jumbled mix I couldn't make sense of right now. Was I so fickle that I could fall in love so soon after losing Andy?

I paced a couple of steps across the floor, hugging my arms close to my body. 'I know I'll have to tell everyone eventually…I just don't know how to do it without looking completely ridiculous.'

'Sometimes the anticipation of something is worse than the actual thing itself,' he said.

I swung back to look at him. 'So why haven't you let everyone in on the secret?'

'It's not my secret to tell.'

I was used to a lifetime of being teased and exploited, of having my weaknesses and flaws broadcast publicly. The fact he hadn't breathed a word of my single status to anyone made something warm spill inside my chest. He'd had a perfect opportunity to make an absolute fool out of me and yet he hadn't done it. Why?

'Want to tell me what happened?' he said.

I let out a long breath. 'I guess, looking back, we'd always had a pretty sketchy sex life. But then I got caught up in the wedding preparations and…well, he got caught up in having an affair with someone more…available.'

I bit my lower lip until it was mostly inside my mouth. I released it, along with a sigh. 'It was the most embarrassing moment of my life and that's saying something because I've had some doozies.'

He closed the distance between us and stroked a wisp of hair off my face. 'My ex was having an affair too. To the guy she's married to now. They'd been friends for years but I didn't realise how friendly until I called on her one night unexpectedly. Simon answered the door. Not a great moment for either of us. I had to give him credit for coming up with an excuse for why he was standing there in nothing but his boxers.'

'What did he say?'

'He was hot.' His mouth gave a rueful little quirk. 'But, then, Helena obviously thought so.'

Behind the humour was lingering hurt. I could see it in his eyes. Or was he like me, and the betrayal was more of a wound to his pride and sense of honour? 'Were you in love with her?'

His mouth twisted again. 'I thought so at the time.'

'And now?'

He stroked his thumb over my bottom lip. 'You read my mother's note.'

I gave him a sheepish look. 'I didn't mean to. It's just I'm a bit of a speed-reader so I took it in at one glance.'

He leaned down and pressed his mouth to mine in a long, warm kiss that sent my senses into chaos. I reached for him automatically, stroking my fingers through his hair.

I leaned into him, relishing in the familiarity of his touch, the naturalness and ease of it.

After a few breathless moments he pulled back to look at me. 'You didn't stay last night.'

'I wasn't sure what the protocol was.'

He frowned a little. 'What do you mean?'

I shrugged beneath the cups of his hands, which were holding the tops of my shoulders. 'I wasn't sure if it was a one-off or...or something else.'

His hands tightened for a moment before he relaxed them, but he didn't let me go. 'You want to go and grab some dinner somewhere after work?'

I bit my lip again as I thought of the implications of us being seen out in public. There was already gossip about him seeing a married woman in the hospital. I hadn't realised until then that my lies were not just hurting me, they had the potential to hurt him. 'Can we just get some takeaway and have it at your place?'

He gave me a levelling look. 'The longer you leave it the worse it's going to be.'

I dipped out of his hold and crossed the floor, hugging my arms to my body again. 'I know. I know. It's just not that simple.'

'It seems simple enough to me.' There was a thread of impatience in his voice. Hard and tight, like a fine wire under strain. 'You just have to be honest, Bertie. People will talk for a while but it'll eventually go away.'

'I need more time.'

'For what?' he said. 'For you to rule out the possibility your ex will come crawling back to you?'

I looked at him in affront. 'You think that's what's stopping me? *Really?*'

His expression was marble cold. 'Be honest with yourself, if not with anyone else.'

'Maybe you should take a lesson from that pulpit you're preaching from,' I threw back.

His eyes were suddenly flinty. 'What's that supposed to mean?'

I flashed him a little glare. 'You've waited for over a year to get involved with someone else. Doesn't that suggest you're still moping over the one who got away?'

He shoved his hands into his trouser pockets as if he was trying to stop himself from reaching for me. 'We haven't got a hope of this progressing past a one-night stand if you don't tell everyone the truth about your situation.'

I drew myself up to my full height, which isn't saying much as I barely came up to the top of his chest. 'I'll tell you why it won't progress past a one-nighter. Because *you* won't allow yourself to feel anything for anyone because you're frightened they'll pull away from you when you least expect it. You'll never give anyone that power again, will you?'

A muscle worked in his jaw. 'I have work to do, so if you've finished listing my faults, I'd appreciate it if you'd let me get on with it.'

I swung away with a haughty toss of my head. Not literally. It was still firmly on my straightened shoulders. 'Fine. I'm out of here.'

I glanced at him when I got to the door but he had already dismissed me. He was sitting behind his desk and scrolling through his emails or whatever was on his computer screen.

CHAPTER ELEVEN

BY THE TIME I got home I'd cooled down, although that might have had something to do with the weather. The snow was falling in earnest and I'd heard on the news they were expecting more overnight. I didn't fancy a long, lonely night alone and I didn't have the enthusiasm for a session of painting and decorating. I looked around the half-painted walls and the threadbare carpets, the tired kitchen with its out-of-date appliances.

My house suddenly looked a bit like my life. A mess.

I was considering what to do about food, not that I had much appetite, when the doorbell rang. I peered through the peephole, toying with the idea of pretending not to be home if it was Margery. It wasn't.

I opened the door and Matt stood there, with snow falling all around him. There was even some clinging to the ends of his eyelashes. He was carrying a bag with takeaway food containers in it and a bottle of wine in a brown paper bag. 'Have we just had our first fight?' he said.

I felt every last residue of anger melt away. 'I'm sorry.'

'No apology necessary.' He held up his peace offering. 'I took a gamble on food. Curry all right?'

'Perfect for a cold winter's night.' I ushered him through to the kitchen. 'I'm sorry the place is a bit of a mess.'

'Was your ex a home handyman?'

I gave him a cynical look. 'Are you joking?'

He frowned. 'You're doing it yourself?'

'I'm trying to…but as you can see it's not going according to plan.' Was it my imagination or did the paint job I'd done the other night look patchy? There was a drip of paint on the skirting board I hadn't noticed before.

'It's a big job for one person.'

'Yes, well, it was supposed to be two people doing it but you know how that turned out.'

He took the wine out of the paper bag. 'You want some help with it?'

I wasn't sure what he was suggesting. But as olive branches went it was a good one—even better than the curry and the wine. 'Don't tell me you're handy with a paintbrush, otherwise I mightn't let you leave.'

He gave a sudden grin. 'I did up my place in Notting Hill before I went to the US. I enjoyed it. It was a change from work, where stuff can't always be fixed.'

I knew exactly what he meant. Sometimes the hopelessness of some patients' situations ate away at me. 'I spent some time with Jason's wife today,' I said, as I handed Matt a couple of wine glasses.

'How's she doing?'

'I think she's struggling a bit, as anyone would in her situation.' I took the glass of wine he had poured for me.

He looked at me across the Formica kitchen table that separated us. 'You're doing a good job. I can see how the things you've set up help. The little touches that make people feel less alienated by the environment.' He waited a beat and then continued, 'I had a brother two years older than me. He died when I was fifteen.'

'I know,' I said. 'Jill told me. She said her sister-in-law is your mother's school friend or something.'

He gave me a quirk of a smile. 'What used to be six degrees of separation is now two with social media.'

I rolled my eyes. 'Tell me about it.'

There was a little silence. I didn't feel so uncomfortable with them now. But after a moment I asked, 'What was it like for you and your parents when Tim was in ICU?'

He looked at the contents of his glass, swirling it as if searching for the memories in the dark cherry-coloured pool. 'Awful. No one told us anything. It was different back then. Doctors didn't always communicate that well with relatives. They only told us what they thought we needed to know. It wasn't enough. My parents thought Tim was going to make it right up until the day he died of pneumonia. It made the grief so much harder for them to cope with. I felt that if only we'd been told from the outset that things were pretty hopeless the grief would have been dealt with earlier. Instead, it's dragged on for years.'

'Grief doesn't have a use-by date.'

'No, I know. But it might've helped my parents prepare themselves a little better.' He put his glass down.

'Did *you* think Tim was going to make it?'

His eyes met mine. 'I hoped he would. I couldn't imagine my life without him. We were close. I looked up to him. He was my role model, the one I turned to for advice or help with homework or whatever. My father was hopeless at that sort of thing. The bottom dropped out of my world when I walked out of the hospital that day. I swore I would do everything I could to make sure other people didn't have to go through that the way we did.'

'So you became an intensive care specialist with a reputation for telling it as it is.'

He gave me a rueful smile. 'That pretty much sums it up.'

I came over to him and touched his shadowed jaw. He hadn't shaved and the stubble caught on the skin of my palm, making something inside my belly shift like a foot slipping on a sheet of black ice. 'Thanks for telling me about Tim. It helps to understand you better.'

He brushed a tendril of hair away from my face. 'I haven't spoken of him in years. It's a no-go area at home. My father goes off his head if Tim's name is mentioned. In his mind the wrong son died.'

'Oh, no, that's terrible,' I said. 'Did he actually *say* that?'

'Only when he's had one too many drinks.'

'Is he an alcoholic?'

'He wouldn't say so, but I have my suspicion he sneaks a few empty bottles into the recycling bin without my mother knowing. Or maybe she does know but keeps quiet because it's not worth the effort of standing up to him or the risk of losing her social standing or both.' His mouth was set back in a grim line. 'God, I *hate* talking about my family. We're not a family any more. Not since Tim died. We're just three people who happen to be related.'

I reached up and smoothed the taut muscles surrounding his tight mouth. 'I'm sorry things have been so tough for you. But look at what you do for others. The way you work so hard, so tirelessly to save lives. So what if you don't have a perfect family? Just wait till you meet mine.'

He smiled and I practically melted on the spot. I watched as his eyes darkened as they went to my mouth, the ink-dark pools of his pupils flaring as he brought his mouth down to mine. His hands buried themselves in my hair, his fingertips sliding along my scalp as he plundered my mouth with feverish intensity. His tongue played with mine, darting and diving and seducing it in a dance that made every cell in my body shudder in delight.

My arms went around his neck, my body pressed so tightly against him I could feel the buttons on his jacket digging into me. I began to undo them, roughly, urgently, impatient to get my hands on him. He shrugged off his jacket and tugged up his jumper and shirt, and I slid my hands along the flat plane of his chest and abdomen. He hauled the garments over his head and they fell to the floor. He set to work on my clothes: my jumper went first, followed by my top and bra. His hands were cold at first on my breasts but they soon warmed as I pressed into his caress.

I tugged at the belt on his trousers, sliding it out of the lugs and letting it slither to the floor. I unzipped him and freed him from his underwear, holding and stroking him as his mouth continued to subject mine to a sensual onslaught that made every hair on my head shiver at the roots.

This was the sort of passion I had been missing in my relationship with Andy. The firestorm of lust and longing that was totally consuming. Before I knew it, Matt had lifted me onto the kitchen counter, parting my thighs so he could come between them. Somehow he'd sourced a condom and got it on before he entered me with a fast, thick thrust that made me whoosh out a breathless gasp.

'You okay?'

Okay? I was in heaven. 'You feel so good,' I said against his mouth, as he came back to kiss me.

He began to move inside me, taking me with him on a roller-coaster ride of passion. Every thrust brought me closer and closer to that final moment of oblivion. It was just frustratingly out of my reach, but then he slid his hands underneath my bottom, lifting my hips just enough to intensify the friction. I came in a cataclysmic storm of sensations that showered and shook and shuddered through me in turn. I felt his own orgasm as it powered through him, the deep quaking of his body and the sharply cut-off groan as he spilled, making my own body respond with another shudder of delight.

He let out a deep, satisfied sigh and leaned his forehead on mine. 'Our dinner is probably cold by now.'

'I don't know,' I said. 'It's pretty hot in this kitchen.'

He smiled against my lips. 'Damn right it is.'

I was walking down my street on my way to work the next morning when I ran into Margery, who was taking Freddy out for a walk. She gave me a look that was colder than the snow that had settled overnight. 'A fine way to behave, I must say,' she said. 'And here I was thinking you were a nice old-fashioned girl. Seems I was wrong.'

'Pardon?'

Her eyes narrowed. 'I saw him.'

My heart gave a little lurch. 'Him?'

'The man who left your house in the early hours of the morning,' she said. 'It wasn't your husband. He wasn't blond and he was much taller.'

I pressed my lips together. How was I going to get out of this? If I told Margery, it would be all over the neighbourhood within minutes. I would have people coming to gawk at me as I walked past their houses. I would be a pariah. I know it's the twenty-first century and all that but people can still be really judgemental about other people's lives.

'Marriage isn't easy, Bertie, take it from me,' she said. 'I was married to my Ralph for thirty-eight years. The first couple of years are always the worst. But what you're doing is plain wrong. What would your patients think if they were to know you were taking men in while your husband is away working in New York?'

I let out a breath that came out in a misty fog. 'The man in question is a friend. Now, if you'll excuse me, I have to get to work.'

Gracie was in the change room when I came in. 'I can't do this any more,' she said. 'It's killing me. I'm so stilted with everyone. I have to keep watching what I say. Everyone thinks I'm cross with them or something.'

'I can't,' I said. 'Can't you see that? It would be social suicide.'

'Don't you mean you won't?' Gracie's look was

accusing. 'This isn't just about you, you know. It's about other people now. Me. Matt Bishop. Your friends and colleagues. The longer you keep this up the more hurt you're going to cause.'

I shoved my things in the locker and closed the door. 'I'm working on it, okay?'

'Then work on it a little faster, will you?' Gracie said, and stormed out.

Jill swivelled around from the computer when I came into the central office. 'Can I have a quick word?'

'Sure.' I tried not to look at my postcard on the noticeboard. I was waiting for the opportunity to come in when no one was around and take it down.

'What's going on between you and Gracie?'

I felt my cheeks flare with heat. 'Nothing. Why?'

She leaned forward and gave me a beady look. 'Sure?'

I controlled every micro-expression on my face. 'Why are you asking?'

'I thought you must have had a squabble or something,' Jill said. 'She's asked for her shifts to be changed so she's not on when you're on. *Have* you got an issue?'

'No, of course not.' I hated myself at that point. Truly hated myself. Gracie might be a relatively new friend but she was loyal and caring. I had dragged her into a nightmare of my own making and now she was doing everything she could to avoid me. It was an uncomfortable reminder of my childhood, where I would be standing alone on one side of the playground while the more popular girls were on the other. I wanted Gracie back on my side but I couldn't do what she asked. I just couldn't.

Jill was still watching me with a contemplative look.

'It wouldn't have anything to do with Matt Bishop, would it?'

I assembled my features into an expression of shocked affront. 'What on earth do you mean?'

'You two have a certain chemistry. Everyone's commenting on it.'

'So?' I said. 'I get on with most people. You do too. It doesn't mean anything illicit is happening.'

'You don't seem happy for someone who's just got married,' Jill said. 'You seem...preoccupied. Is everything all right between you and your husband?'

I clenched my hands instead of my teeth because that would be less audible. 'What is this? Why is everyone so fascinated with my private life?'

Jill tapped her fingertips on her knees. 'Bertie, this gossip that's going around is not doing Matt any favours with the management team. The CEO is talking about terminating his contract.'

I frowned. 'On what grounds? His private life is no one's business!'

She gave me a worldly look. 'You know how conservative the hospital management team is. They're concerned about the image of the hospital.'

'They should be concerned about the welfare of the patients and less with the private lives of their staff,' I threw back.

'I'm just saying—'

'Haven't people got better things to do than gossip?' I said.

Jill let out a sigh and turned back to the computer.

I stared at her back for a moment. I trusted Gracie but I didn't know Jill well enough to share my secret with her. I hated it that she thought I was a cheating wife but what else could I do? If I told her, I'd have to tell everyone. I wasn't prepared to do that. I had a plan. I was going to activate it. There was a way around this. I would resign and find another placement. Problem solved.

'I'm sorry, Jill, it's just things are a little difficult for me right now. I'm finding it hard to settle back in after being on my...on leave.'

She tapped a few keys before turning around again. 'Marriage is hard work. Just be careful, okay?'

I didn't see Matt at work because I did everything in my power to avoid being seen by him or with him. Thankfully I had other duties that kept me out of ICU for most of the day. I finally left for home after some overtime in Theatre when Stuart's list got blown out with a complication. I was walking out of the hospital when I saw Matt's tall figure coming towards me. He must have been waiting for me to come through the front exit. I pretended not to notice him and kept my head down.

'Bertie?'

'Don't draw attention to us,' I said, out of the side of my mouth.

'I thought I'd walk you home.'

'Please, don't,' I said, huddling further into my coat.

'We need to talk.'

'Not here. There are CCTV cameras everywhere.' I sounded completely paranoid. But, then, I was. Completely and utterly paranoid. Were the curtains twitching on every floor as staff and patients looked down at us or was I just imagining it?

Matt took me by the arm and turned me to face him. 'Listen to me.'

I was overwrought with the stress of it all. Gracie, Jill, the thought of Matt losing his job over my stupidity. I looked into his eyes and saw what he was going to say before he said it. And there I'd been, thinking my mum was the only one who could read minds. 'I know what you're going to say.'

'Bertie, you have to choose.'

'Choose what?' I pretended I didn't know what he meant. But really I was just delaying the pain. I couldn't have him and my secret. I had to make a choice.

His expression was gravely serious. 'If we're going to go somewhere with this relationship then you have to tell everyone the truth.'

'I thought you said you weren't interested in a relationship. You said you had other priorities.'

His eyes were implacable as they held mine. 'I'm not going to lose my job because you're too immature to face up to what you should've faced before Christmas.'

I glared at him. 'That's rich, coming from you! You took a whole year to get over what's-her-name.'

His jaw tightened like a clamp. 'We're not talking about me. We're talking about you.'

'I'm going to put in my resignation,' I said. 'I'll move to another hospital where no one knows about Andy. You and I can still see each other and no one will ever—'

'Will you listen to yourself?' he said, his eyes dark and glittering with disdain. 'What are you, fourteen?'

I stiffened my spine. 'Fine. I'll accept your ultimatum.'

He shook his head at me. 'Don't do this, sweetheart.'

I put up my chin. 'I'm not throwing my professional reputation away for a fling. I'm fine with it ending. I never wanted it in the first place.'

'You've made lying into an art form,' he said, with a cutting edge to his voice. 'But when you get home and start lying to the person you're looking at in the mirror, you'll know you're really in trouble.'

I was in trouble from the moment I laid eyes on him, but now was hardly the time to tell him. I was trying to salvage what was left of my pride. 'It's over, Matt. It was fun—or at least it was for you—while it lasted.'

'I didn't sleep with you to make fun of you,' he said. 'I slept with you because I…' He stopped and shoved a hand through his hair.

I raised a cynically arched eyebrow. 'Because you…?'

He dropped his hand. His mask was back in place. For a moment there I'd thought I'd seen a glimmer of pain in his gaze but it was well and truly gone now. I figured I'd probably imagined it. 'Never mind.'

'I have one question,' I said. 'Why did you ask me to take over the planning of the ball?'

He let out a long breath. 'I thought it would help you get over your break-up. I thought it would give you something to distract you. But if you don't want to follow through with it, I'll find someone else.'

'I'm sure it won't take you too long to find a replacement,' I shot back.

He gave me another I'm-over-this look and turned away and walked back through the front doors of the hospital.

* * *

I typed up my resignation that night and printed it out and signed it with a flourish. I looked at it for a long time before I folded it and slid it into an envelope. I left it lying on the desk—I don't have any helpful house-keeping staff so there was no prospect of it being posted until I was ready to do so myself.

Jason's parents asked to speak to me when I got to ICU the next day. They were waiting in my relatives' room but I hadn't had time to turn on the essential oil infuser as I'd been caught up on the ward. Ken Ryder was hold-ing his wife, Maggie's, hand. Megan was still by Jason's bedside. I'd caught a glimpse of her on my way past, crying as she held one of his hands.

'We want the truth,' Ken said. 'Mr McTaggart is say-ing one thing. Dr Bishop is saying another. We want your opinion. What's our son's prognosis?'

I looked at their haggard faces, their drawn and tired features. The shadows, in and under their eyes, and the lines on their faces that had seemed to deepen like trenches by the end of each long, heartbreaking day. I took a deep breath, feeling as if I was stepping out of a part of my personality like someone taking off a warm, thick coat. I felt exposed and vulnerable without it but I could no longer hide beneath its comforting folds. 'There's a very real possibility Jason will never recover.'

Saying the words felt like speaking a different lan-guage, one without hope as part of its vocabulary. I watched as Jason's parents took them in. It wasn't the first time they'd heard them but hearing it from me—

the one person who had offered them hope and positive thinking from the get-go—was clearly devastating.

'I'm sorry,' I said, blinking back tears. I never cried at work. I was always so self-contained but I could no longer keep that professional distance. In that small, private room I became Bertie instead of Dr Clark. I hugged Jason's parents and offered what comfort I could but it wasn't enough. It could never be enough because I could not—no matter how hard I tried—bring back their boy.

Jem had a student-free day that coincided with my next day off so she met me in Knightsbridge for lunch in one of our favourite haunts. 'So, what gives?' she said, when she noticed I wasn't eating my steak with any of my usual gusto.

I stabbed a French fry but didn't bring it up to my mouth. 'Don't want to talk about it.'

Jem reached over and pinched one of my fries. She had already finished all hers. She has this amazing ability to eat loads of food without putting on an ounce. I should hate her for it. 'You're in love with him.'

I pulled back my chin against my chest. 'With Andy?'

'No, you goose,' she said. 'With this Matt guy.'

'Don't be ridiculous. I've only known him, what, three and a half weeks? That's not long enough to fall in love.'

'Don't bet on it.'

I raised my brows. 'The Sicilian guy?'

Jem got that stony, closed-off look on her face. 'We're not talking about me. We're talking about you.'

Why are all the people in my life saying the same

thing? I wondered. 'Everyone is talking about me. Or at least they will be when my resignation hits the HR department tomorrow.'

Jem frowned. 'You're resigning?'

'What else can I do?'

She gave me one of her big-sister, older-and-wiser looks. 'What about your project?'

'I've got enough data to go on with and once I get a new placement I'll set it up again.' Even as I said it I realised how difficult it would be. I had developed a high level of trust at St Iggy's, which was why Jeffrey Hooper had allowed me to be so innovative. I might not find the same enthusiasm in another hospital.

Jem filched another fry. 'What about the St Valentine's ball? Aren't you the one organising that?'

I felt a twinge of guilt at how I'd walked away from my responsibilities. I'd heard Matt had found someone to take over—a nurse from the cardiac unit. I wondered with another pang if he was seeing her outside work. 'I was but it's been handed to someone else. I can do without the stress on top of everything else. Anyway, I haven't got a costume.'

'You could always go as yourself.'

I gave her a droll look. 'Ha, ha.'

'What about your neighbours?' Jem wiped her fingers on her napkin. 'You're not thinking of moving too, are you?'

I was ashamed to admit I was. I was even thinking about emigrating. No one would be able to gossip about me then. *Siberia should just about do it*, I thought. 'None of them are talking to me. Clearly Margery's been busy.'

Jem leaned across the table and patted my hand. 'Never mind. At least she won't be asking you to mind her horrible little dog any more.'

'Like she should throw the first stone,' I said. 'Her Freddy humps anything that's—' I stopped speaking when I saw the colour leave Jem's face. She was looking at the entrance of the restaurant, her eyes widening with horror. 'What's wrong?' I said.

She grabbed the bill the waitress had left moments earlier and thrust it at me. 'Do you mind getting this? I'll meet you in Harrods at the chocolate counter.'

'But—'

I frowned as I watched her slip out the back way through the kitchen. Then I turned and looked at the tall, stunningly handsome Italian man walking in with a beautiful blonde woman by his side.

It seemed I wasn't the only coward in the family after all.

CHAPTER TWELVE

MY RESIGNATION CAUSED quite a stir amongst the staff when I came in the day after it had been lodged. I had to dodge a few twisty questions, including one about whether I was pregnant. Gracie kept giving me looks I stubbornly refused to acknowledge. It was all right lecturing me about telling the truth but she wasn't the one who'd have had to live down the ignominy of pretending to be married. It was easier this way. I was making a new start and in a few months no one would even remember me.

My heart gave a painful squeeze when I walked past Matt's office. I hadn't seen him other than in passing since our conversation in the car park. I wondered if he was feeling even half the distress I was. The thought of not seeing him again was like leaving a part of myself behind. A part I'd only just discovered. I hadn't realised I was in love with him until I'd lost him. I guess it had crept up on me. Each kiss, each touch, each time we'd made love a bit more of my heart had been won over.

But if he loved me then surely he wouldn't have made me choose. It was his reputation he was most concerned about, not me. It proved what a fool I'd been to allow our relationship to get to that stage. Hadn't he said from the start he had other priorities right now? I had foolishly agreed to getting involved and now I was paying the price.

But if he'd only wanted a casual fling why had he revealed so much to me about his past? It wasn't just the red-hot passion I longed for in a relationship. It was that wonderful sense of intimacy, of being able to talk about painful things without fear of judgement or lack of interest. Matt had opened up to me in the same way I had opened up to him. Why, then, had he made me choose? It wasn't fair to push me. To blackmail me.

I was getting my things out of the central office on my last day when Jill came in with a bundle of files to be entered into the computer. 'I can't believe you're not coming to the ball,' she said. 'Why not use it as a send-off? We haven't had time to do a drinks thing for you or anything.'

'I don't want any fuss,' I said, eyeing that wretched postcard. If only I could get it off that board then maybe my life would magically return to normal, or whatever normal for me was.

'This all seems rather sudden,' Jill said. 'Did the CEO pressure you to leave or something?'

'No, of course not,' I said. 'It was my decision.'

She eyed me doubtfully for a moment. 'It won't be the same here without you, Bertie. You've brought a lot of fun to the department. Even Stuart is saying how much he's going to miss you. And Prof Cleary. Do you know what he said? He said you're like a bright red poppy in a field of oats.'

I blinked back a sting of tears. 'That was sweet of him.'

There was a short silence.

'You weren't really having an affair with Matt Bishop, were you?' Jill asked.

I couldn't hold her look and turned to the notice-board and unpinned the postcard. 'You don't mind if I take this?'

'Of course not,' she said. 'It'll just get thrown out. You might as well keep it for sentimental value.'

I pasted a tight smile on my face. 'That's what I thought.'

I felt like Cinderella on the night of the ball, except I didn't have two ugly stepsisters and a horrid stepmother keeping me away. I was keeping myself away. I watched as the clock ticked towards midnight. I imagined all the guests arriving, walking up the red carpet, couples arm in arm. My stomach clenched at the thought of Matt arriving with some gorgeous date on his arm. I thought of him dancing with her, his arms around her as I'd dreamed of his around me. I hadn't even had the chance to see if we could actually dance.

But if our lovemaking was anything to go by, I thought we would've had a chance to be *that* couple on the dance floor. You know, the couple you see at weddings or functions who look like they've just come off a reality dance show, their movements together so beautifully synchronised it was spellbinding to watch. I wanted us to be that couple. We were a great team at work. We balanced each other out. Matt's cold, hard science needed softening with my more feelings-based intuition. We were like a perfect cocktail. The flavours by themselves weren't too flash, but put them together and, wham. What a knockout combination.

I looked at the clock again. The ball didn't end until one a.m. If I got my skates on I would have just enough time to poke my head in the door to see if everything had gone according to plan. I was deeply ashamed at not following through with my commitment. People had been relying on me and I'd walked off the job. What if not enough money was raised, or what if there was some last-minute hitch and I wasn't there to sort it out? Since when had I become a quitter? I still had my ticket and I had a choice of costumes from previous fancy-dress parties. It was a choice between Princess Fiona from *Shrek* or Kermit the Frog.

I didn't fancy being either so I decided to do what Jem had suggested. I pulled out a nineteen-fifties ball gown I'd bought for twenty pounds in a charity shop a few years ago. I'd never worn it in public because I'd always thought it was too glamorous for me. But when I put it on and looked at myself in the mirror it was like looking at myself for the first time.

I put my hair up and put on a bit of make-up. I spritzed myself with perfume and picked up a little drawstring evening purse that matched the white organza of my gown. Actually, it wasn't really white any more. It was more of an off-white, leaning towards yellowed with age, and it had a couple of moth holes in the flared skirt, but I was hoping no one would notice that. I slipped on some heels and prayed my toes would forgive me for the ensuing torture.

I called a cab—there weren't any pumpkin coaches on duty that night—and went to the hotel.

The ball was in full swing when I slipped in to stand by one of the red-rose arrangements with heart-shaped helium balloons sticking out of it. The dance floor was full of dancers in a variety of costumes. Some had taken the fun aspect of the night to extremes but there was a nice sprinkling of elegance amongst the frivolity.

I saw Matt dancing with one of the nurses from A and E. My heart gave a painful spasm as I saw his hand in the small of her back as they waltzed around the dance floor. They looked so good together. Not quite as good as a couple from a dance show…in fact, I thought I saw Matt tread on her toe at one point but that could've been my wishful thinking in overdrive. But then, as if he had a sixth sense, he suddenly stopped dancing and said something to his partner. She nodded and slipped away to dance with someone else.

Then he turned and met my gaze across the crowded room.

I know it sounds like a cliché but I felt my heart come to a standstill. Tears sprouted in my eyes as he came towards me. He was dressed in an old-style tuxedo with a red rosebud pinned to his lapel—no silly cartoon or superhero characters for him. He took my evening-gloved hands in his. 'So Cinderella made it after all,' he said.

'Yes…a close call but so far my glass slippers are intact.'

'Dance with me?'

He didn't give me time to say yay or nay. Suddenly I was in his arms and we were moving around the dance floor. Yes, you guessed it. Just like one of *those* couples. In fact, we were so good everyone else stopped dancing to look at us. I would have enjoyed it more if I hadn't realised there were two reasons they were staring. One: we were pretty fantastic together. Two: I was still pretending to be married to someone else.

It was exactly five minutes to midnight.

I stopped dancing and slipped out of Matt's hold. 'Will you excuse me for a moment?' I said. 'There's something I have to do.'

Everyone was still standing on the perimeter of the dance floor as I walked over to the podium, where a microphone had been positioned for the fundraising auction that had been conducted earlier. I waited for the musicians to stop playing the last bars of their song and then I took a deep breath. 'Hi,' I said, waving to all of the familiar faces and the not-so-familiar ones.

'For those of you who don't know, I'm Bertie Clark.' I felt like someone at a support group owning up to some sort of vice. 'There's something I have to confess. I'm not really married. I was jilted the night before the wedding. I didn't mean to send that postcard. That sort of happened by accident. I've been pretending ever since. I'm sorry for all the hurt I've caused. It was stupid and immature and I'm terribly, unreservedly, unequivocally sorry.' I thought I'd better stop there. I was starting to sound like a thesaurus.

There was a moment of stunned silence and then everyone gave me a round of applause as they started to surge forward on the dance floor. I felt like a rock star at a concert. I wondered if I should take a bow or do an encore or something. It was almost worth all the angst of the last few weeks to be the centre of attention in such a celebratory way. Almost.

I saw Matt carve his way through the crowd towards me. I stepped down off the podium and straight into his open arms. 'So proud of you, sweetheart,' he said. 'So very proud.'

'This doesn't mean I'm coming back to work at St Iggy's,' I said.

'That's a shame as there's a patient who's pretty keen to see you,' he said, with an excited twinkle in his blue-grey eyes.

Something lifted inside my chest like a sudden up-draught of air. 'Jason's awake?'

Matt grinned. 'I got a call from the registrar half an hour ago. Megan was reading *Chicken Little* to him and he opened his eyes and spoke a couple of words.'

I threw my arms around him and danced up and down on the spot. 'That's the best news! I'm so thrilled for him, for all of them.'

Matt swung me around in his arms so high that my dress ballooned out in an organza circle. I was glad I'd put on my best knickers as everyone was probably getting a good eyeful of them. 'I swore I would never do this in public, but will you marry me?' he said.

I hadn't realised until that point the ballroom was completely and utterly quiet. You could have heard a pin drop. Or maybe that was my jaw hitting the floor. I blinked and opened and shut my mouth a couple of times. 'What did you say?'

He smiled that dancing smile that always made my insides turn over. 'I know it's too early to be propos-ing. How long's it been, four weeks? But I don't see the point in wasting months and years waiting to ask you. I love you. I fell in love with you that first day in my office when you stood up to me with your beauti-ful brown eyes flashing.'

I looked at him in stunned amazement. 'You love me?'

'I adore you,' he said. 'I love everything about you. I love the way you screw up your nose and twitch like a rabbit when you're stressed. I love the way you never gave up hope on Jason. I love the way you fight for what you believe in. You're wacky and a little crazy and I never know what to expect when I see you because you wear such way-out clothes, but I want to see you every day for the rest of my life. I want to have babies with you. I want us to be a family together. So will you do it? Will you marry me?'

'You love me...' I said it as if I was dreaming and that someone was going to tap me on the shoulder any minute and tell me to snap out of it.

Someone did tap me on the shoulder. It was Gracie. 'Congratulations,' she said, with a huge smile.

'But I haven't given him my answer,' I said.

The crowd began to applaud again, louder and louder, and there was a fair bit of foot-stomping as well. Even the band joined in with a big theatrical drum roll.

Then everything went absolutely quiet again and it was as if it were just Matt and I in that room. It was like we were the only people left on the planet. I saw the love he had for me shining in his eyes. I felt it in his touch as he tenderly brushed back a stray tendril of my hair from my face. I felt it in the energy that passed from his body to mine where we touched thigh to thigh, chest to chest, heart to heart.

I smiled a smile that felt like it was splitting my face in two. 'Yes,' I said, and then his mouth came down and met mine.

* * * * *

MILLS & BOON®
Hardback – February 2015

ROMANCE

The Redemption of Darius Sterne	Carole Mortimer
The Sultan's Harem Bride	Annie West
Playing by the Greek's Rules	Sarah Morgan
Innocent in His Diamonds	Maya Blake
To Wear His Ring Again	Chantelle Shaw
The Man to Be Reckoned With	Tara Pammi
Claimed by the Sheikh	Rachael Thomas
Delucca's Marriage Contract	Abby Green
Her Brooding Italian Boss	Susan Meier
The Heiress's Secret Baby	Jessica Gilmore
A Pregnancy, a Party & a Proposal	Teresa Carpenter
Best Friend to Wife and Mother?	Caroline Anderson
The Sheikh Doctor's Bride	Meredith Webber
A Baby to Heal Their Hearts	Kate Hardy
One Hot Desert Night	Kristi Gold
Snowed In with Her Ex	Andrea Laurence
Cowgirls Don't Cry	Silver James
Terms of a Texas Marriage	Lauren Canan

MEDICAL

A Date with Her Valentine Doc	Melanie Milburne
It Happened in Paris...	Robin Gianna
Temptation in Paradise	Joanna Neil
The Surgeon's Baby Secret	Amber McKenzie

0115 GEN STD HB

MILLS & BOON®
Large Print – February 2015

ROMANCE

An Heiress for His Empire	Lucy Monroe
His for a Price	Caitlin Crews
Commanded by the Sheikh	Kate Hewitt
The Valquez Bride	Melanie Milburne
The Uncompromising Italian	Cathy Williams
Prince Hafiz's Only Vice	Susanna Carr
A Deal Before the Altar	Rachael Thomas
The Billionaire in Disguise	Soraya Lane
The Unexpected Honeymoon	Barbara Wallace
A Princess by Christmas	Jennifer Faye
His Reluctant Cinderella	Jessica Gilmore

HISTORICAL

Zachary Black: Duke of Debauchery	Carole Mortimer
The Truth About Lady Felkirk	Christine Merrill
The Courtesan's Book of Secrets	Georgie Lee
Betrayed by His Kiss	Amanda McCabe
Falling for Her Captor	Elisabeth Hobbes

MEDICAL

Tempted by Her Boss	Scarlet Wilson
His Girl From Nowhere	Tina Beckett
Falling For Dr Dimitriou	Anne Fraser
Return of Dr Irresistible	Amalie Berlin
Daring to Date Her Boss	Joanna Neil
A Doctor to Heal Her Heart	Annie Claydon

MILLS & BOON®
Hardback – March 2015

ROMANCE

The Taming of Xander Sterne	Carole Mortimer
In the Brazilian's Debt	Susan Stephens
At the Count's Bidding	Caitlin Crews
The Sheikh's Sinful Seduction	Dani Collins
The Real Romero	Cathy Williams
His Defiant Desert Queen	Jane Porter
Prince Nadir's Secret Heir	Michelle Conder
Princess's Secret Baby	Carol Marinelli
The Renegade Billionaire	Rebecca Winters
The Playboy of Rome	Jennifer Faye
Reunited with Her Italian Ex	Lucy Gordon
Her Knight in the Outback	Nikki Logan
Baby Twins to Bind Them	Carol Marinelli
The Firefighter to Heal Her Heart	Annie O'Neil
Thirty Days to Win His Wife	Andrea Laurence
Her Forbidden Cowboy	Charlene Sands
The Blackstone Heir	Dani Wade
After Hours with Her Ex	Maureen Child

MEDICAL

Tortured by Her Touch	Dianne Drake
It Happened in Vegas	Amy Ruttan
The Family She Needs	Sue MacKay
A Father for Poppy	Abigail Gordon

A
Th
Pro
O
To
T
T
A
A

h
de
D